CHARMCASTERS AND THE MYSTERIOUS ARTIFACT

MORE FROM MANSWELL T
PETERSON

Locrottum Academy Series

- Locrottum Academy Book 1
- Locrottum Academy Book 2
- Locrottum Academy Book 3
- Locrottum Academy Book 4
- Locrottum Academy Book 5
- Locrottum Academy Book 6

Charmcasters Academy Series

- Charmcasters and the Mysterious Artifact

CHARMCASTERS AND THE MYSTERIOUS ARTIFACT

CHARMCASTERS ACADEMY
BOOK ONE

MANSWELL T PETERSON

OMEGAMAN PUBLISHING

To Braylen...
keep believing in magic and everything that makes you
happy. You are a true inspiration to me and I'm proud
to be your dad.

Manswell T Peterson

CHAPTER ONE

Elara Silverwind stirred in her sleep. The sun's early rays crept through a gap in her curtains. Her dreams, filled with swirling gusts of wind and the promise of adventure, dissipated as she blinked open her eyes. The morning light glinted off a shimmering envelope that seemed to materialize out of thin air, drawing Elara's attention as it floated gracefully through the room.

"An acceptance letter..." she whispered to herself, rubbing her eyes to ensure she wasn't still dreaming.

Fourteen-year-old Elara is a girl of slight stature, but she's a thunderstorm packed into a teacup. Her hair tumbled down her back in a cascade of silver that gleamed like starlight whenever she used her magic. She had eyes as blue as an azure sky, a perfect mirror to her wind-wielding prowess. And Elara's parents are the first to admit that her personality is a whirlwind of tenacity, persistence, and loyalty. Those same traits brought her to this very moment.

A moment to decide if she has a future as a Charmcaster.

As if summoned by her thoughts, the letter drifted downward, releasing a burst of iridescent sparkles that danced around her head like a halo. The magical display was mesmerizing, but Elara's focus remained on the strange, hovering envelope. With her heart racing, she reached out a trembling hand and grasped it.

"Please, be good news," she murmured, feeling the weight of the thick parchment between her fingers.

Elara sat back against the pillows and took in her bedroom, adorned in shades of blue and silver. They lined the walls with bookshelves filled with volumes of magic, adventure, and ancient legends. Her desk, tucked beneath a window offering a view of the backyard garden, was cluttered with pencils, books, and notebook paper—the casualties of many late-night cram sessions.

Her most prized possessions were the glittering gold and silver wind chimes that hung in every corner of the room, crafted from whimsical glass, metal, and wood. The chimes dangled from every possible nook, singing their unique melodies with every gust of wind magic Elara invoked. They were more than just decorations; they were a constant reminder of Elara's affinity for the wind element—a talent she hoped to hone at the academy.

If the school accepted her.

As Elara held the envelope in her hands, she wavered. What if it wasn't an acceptance letter? What if all her dreams were about to shatter like fragile glass? She bit her lip, considering the possibility of rejection. She could feel the faintest brush of wind rustle her hair, as if her own magic was urging her to face the truth hidden within the envelope.

"Here I go," she whispered, her voice barely audible as she slid her finger beneath the wax seal, breaking it open carefully.

As soon as Elara glimpsed the "*Congratulations!*" at the top of the acceptance letter, a squeal of delight escaped her lips. She jumped out of bed, still in her nightgown embossed with puffy white clouds. Elara clutched the letter tightly to her chest, trying not to wrinkle the precious invitation. The magic within her swirled about the room, performing off her joy and excitement.

"Blessed by the four winds!" she exclaimed, her laughter the sound of tinkling bells.

As if on cue, the wind chimes hanging in her room swayed gently, singing their own unique melody, adding to the celebration of the moment.

"Accepted... I've really been accepted!" she said, unable to contain her glee.

The realization of learning more about her magical abilities by attending the prestigious *Charmcaster Academy of Magic and Elements* on Mythos Isle filled Elara's heart with hope and eagerness.

"Thank you!" she whispered to the winds.

As the last of her wind chimes settled, Elara took a deep breath. It was time for her true adventure to begin.

The door to Elara's bedroom didn't just open—it swung wide open—presenting her parents like a hurricane. Her dad, Asher Silverwind, was a sturdy tower of a man with a mane of salt-and-pepper hair. He donned a rumpled T-shirt, plaid pajama bottoms, and cozy slippers, with a familiar grin resting on his lips—a smile that made Elara feel like they shared a private joke.

Her mom, Lyra Silverwind, glided into the room with grace and radiance, her golden tresses streaming around her delicate features. Dressed in a chic white blouse, paired with her well-loved jeans, she padded around on bare feet as though the floor was her personal dance stage. Her blue eyes—mirrors of Elara's own—sparkled with a curiosity that was both infectious and slightly mischievous. The room seemed to shimmer with her parents' shared anticipation. The wind chimes chattering as if to add their congratulations, too.

"Mom, Dad!" Elara cried, waving the acceptance letter in the air. "I got in! I've been accepted to the academy!"

Her parents exchanged glances, joy brimming in their eyes as they rushed to their daughter. Her father ruffled Elara's hair affectionately, while her mother wrapped her arms around her daughter tightly.

"Congratulations, dearest!" her mother exclaimed. "We knew you could do it."

"Without a doubt," her father agreed, his chest swelling with pride. "You are destined for greatness, Elara. Your mother and I are so very, very proud of you."

As her parents showered her with praise, Elara felt warmth spread through her body, her heart overflowing with happiness. She knew how much this moment meant to them—not only because her parents had both attended the same academy themselves but also because they understood the depth of her passion for magic and her desire to become a master wind elemental.

"I'm so excited!" Elara said, her voice thick with emotion. "I was so afraid it would be a rejection."

"Not a chance." Her father placed a comforting hand on her shoulder, his expression sincere and full of wisdom. "Keep in mind, Elara, the academy is tough, but we know you have the strength and resolve to face any challenges that come your way."

Elara nodded, her resolve reaffirmed by her father. With her parents by her side and the wind at her command, she was ready to take on the academy—and nothing would stand in her way.

"This is a special day, Elara." Her mother gushed as she sat down on the bed beside her daughter. "You'll be attending the same academy as your father, and I did."

Her father joined them, taking a seat on Elara's other side, his voice full of pride. "And you're going to love Mythos Isle."

"Is the island really as magical as they say?" Elara asked, clutching her acceptance letter in her lap.

"Even more so," Mother replied. "The island itself is steeped in ancient magic, and the school's library holds secrets you can't even begin to imagine."

"Your mother's right," Father added. "And don't

forget about the wonderful friends you'll make there. Magical bonds forged at Charmcaster Academy will last a lifetime."

As Elara listened to her parents reminisce, a bout of wonderment bubbled within her, causing a gust of wind to whirl around the room again and flutter her hair. The collection of wind chimes hanging near her window tinkled softly, like applause.

"Elara, baby girl, try to control your wind magic when you're excited," her mother soothingly reminded her, a fond smile on her lips.

"Sorry, Mom." Elara quickly reigned in her emotions and stilled the surrounding air.

"Speaking of wind magic," her father said, "you'll have the opportunity to learn from the greatest Charmcaster professors. Your talent for wind manipulation will truly flourish there."

"Really?" Elara's eyes widened. "I can't wait to learn everything there is to know about wind magic! I want to become a master of the winds!"

"Your determination has always been one of your strongest qualities, sweetie," her mother said, brushing a strand of silver hair behind Elara's ear. "Just take into account that magic is a gift, and with it comes great responsibility."

"Of course, Mom." Elara rolled her eyes. "I'm not

Spiderman, and this isn't a comic. It's real life!" She almost lost control again, and one wind chime swayed. But she caught herself before Mother noticed.

"Don't sass your mom, kiddo." Her father smirked as he patted the top of her head. "I'm going to make us a celebratory breakfast," her father said, standing up from Elara's bed. "You should start packing." With that, Elara's father left the room, his footsteps echoing down the hallway.

Her mother smiled and called after him, "Meet you in the kitchen when we're done, sweetheart."

Once they were alone, Elara and her mother started packing her belongings. Elara's mother opened the closet and wheeled out a large suitcase and an old steamer trunk. Together, they began filling them with Elara's belongings. Yes, they could use magic to all of it, but Elara wanted to indulge in some alone time with her mother. Knowing that soon she would miss her like crazy. Maybe even miss her so much she can't sleep or eat. As Mother went through a pile of clothing, Elara stuffed some books and knick-knacks into the trunk. All the while, she kept glancing at her mom folding dresses and fitting them into the suitcase. A light hum, perhaps a lullaby, was barely audible from mother.

"Mom, tell me more about the classes at the academy," Elara asked as she bounced on the bed. One shoe hopping out of the suitcase as she landed.

"Ah, where to begin?" Her mother mused, a nostalgic grin creeping across her face. "You'll be a first-year student, so you will study the Fundamentals of Charmcasting, among other things."

While Elara listened intently to her mother's words, she folded shirts into neat little piles and arranged them inside the suitcase. "That sounds fascinating." Elara tucked a few pairs of shoes in around the clothes, grabbing the one that tried to get away.

"It certainly is," her mother replied as she filled the trunk with Elara's collection of unused journals and sketchbooks. "Your specialty will be in Weather Magic and Manipulation taught by Professor Mistral, who's a popular teacher at the academy. Then there's Elemental Magic, where you'll study all four of the traditional elements: earth, fire, and water. I wonder if the kids still tease each other with name calling. Airhead, hot stuff. Just ignore them. It just means they're jealous."

Elara fidgeted with a strand of her hair. "Mom, I know kids can be mean. But I am not even worried about that. I am, so like, super thrilled about going to school. But I feel like I got these crazy butterflies fluttering around in my stomach," she admits to her mother, bringing a soft rosy hue to her cheeks.

"That's normal, baby girl. The academy will be a huge adjustment, but you'll grow to love it there," her mother said gently. "And we can write letters. Unfortunately, there is no cell service or internet on the island."

"I know, Mom," Elara replied with a hint of disappointment. "No cell service or internet? So it's like living in the dark ages? Cool. I guess. But hey, at least we'll have handwritten letters. It'll be like our own magical communication network, right?"

"Right. We can pretend we are royals living in far-off lands because of a war." Mother let out a little giggle, making Elara a little homesick already. After a second of silence, "Promise me you'll write to us often," her mother said, her gaze filled with affection. "We want to hear all about your adventures and studies while you're there."

"I promise to write once a week," Elara responded earnestly, her heart expanding with love and gratitude for her family. Without them, she wouldn't be here with this amazing opportunity.

"Good." Her mother folded a sweater and laid it in the suitcase. "I hope that doesn't take up too much room. You won't need much as far as cold weather clothing goes."

"Did you like the academy?" Elara asked, eager to know more.

"Oh, yes, very much. Charmcaster Academy has four dorms for each student year that represent a certain season. The summer dorm are quarters for first-year students, like you, the autumn dorm is for second-year students, the winter dorms accommodate the third-year students, and the spring dorm is a residence for fourth-year students."

"Wow, I can't wait to meet my dorm-mate!" Elara said. Then, kissing the nose of her teddy bear, she stuffed him into the large trunk. "Did you like your roommate?"

"Your father and I had our fair share of challenges during our time at Charmcaster Academy," her mother remarked, her gaze distant as she reminisced. "But we made lifelong friends and learned invaluable lessons. Looking back, I realize I was hardly ever in my room except to sleep, but yes, my roommates were easy enough to live with." With a look of satisfaction, her mother placed the last of Elara's clothing pile into the suitcase.

Her mother gave Elara a comforting squeeze around her shoulders. "We're so proud of you, baby girl. Now, let's finish this packing so we can enjoy some of your father's delicious breakfast."

"I will definitely miss Dad's cooking." Elara and her mother nodded together.

Elara directed her energy toward the scattered objects in her room, urging the wind to lift them and place them carefully into the trunk. With a gentle sway, her clothes folded themselves and nestled into every available space. Her books floated off the shelves, their pages dancing as they gracefully settled atop the neatly packed clothing.

As she directed the subtle gusts of wind, Elara felt a pang of sadness. The thought of leaving her parents behind, even for the wondrous education that awaited her at Charmcaster Academy, weighed heavily on her heart. She knew this was an opportunity she couldn't pass up, but parting with her family would be painful.

"Working your magic, I see," her mother commented as she observed Elara's wind-woven packing.

Elara nodded, swallowing the lump in her throat. "I'll miss you and Dad so much," she whispered, her eyes glistening with unshed tears as they stood in the doorway.

"Hey, we'll always be here for you," her mother reassured her, wrapping her arms around Elara and embracing her daughter tight. "And just think of all the amazing things you'll learn and the friends you'll make. Besides, we're only a letter away."

"Thanks, Mom." Elara hugged her back, taking comfort in her mother's warmth.

With her belongings packed and her thoughts swirling like the wind she commanded, Elara followed her mother down the stairs to the kitchen, where her father laid out a bountiful spread of pancakes and sausages. The enticing aroma filled the air as they sat down together, a momentary reprieve from the emotions threatening to overwhelm Elara.

Everyone gathered around the rustic kitchen table surrounded by four mismatched chairs and a colorful rag rug underneath, steam rising from their breakfast of pancakes and savory sausage. They adorn the walls with cheerful floral prints and a few hand-painted ceramic plates. A small stove and an old-fashioned refrigerator sat tucked away in the corner of the room.

"Dig in!" Her father said enthusiastically, pouring orange juice from a glass pitcher into Elara's cup. "We need to celebrate your acceptance to the academy properly!"

"Thanks, Dad." Elara picked up her fork and knife and cut slices of the fluffy golden-brown pancakes before taking a bite. The flavor of her father's cooking filled her mouth, and she smiled.

As they ate, Elara's parents reminisced about their own experiences at the school and life on Mythos Isle. The light streamed in through the windows, reflecting off the warm, honey-toned wood panel walls. Her father recalled the time he accidentally summoned a miniature tornado during a wind magic lesson, while her mother sipped her juice as she talked about her first encounter with a lunar nymph in the enchanted gardens. She gestured flamboyantly while recounting the story, making the family burst into laughter.

"Remember," her father mumbled around a mouthful of pancake, "if you encounter a mischievous pixie, don't let them borrow your socks. They have a tendency to vanish into thin air."

Elara giggled, her laughter blending with the clinking of cutlery. Her mother snickered, her eyes twinkling with amusement.

Her father wiped his mouth with a napkin and leaned closer to Elara, a mischievous grin on his face. "And don't forget, if you happen to stumble upon a magical talking squirrel, be sure to ask them for their secret acorn stash."

Elara nodded, a playful gleam in her eyes. "I'll keep that in mind, Dad. No sock loans to pixies and secret acorns from squirrels. Got it."

Mother raised her glass of juice and toasted, "No to pixies, yes to acorns!"

Her parents erupted into laughter, the joyful sound filling the room and warming Elara's heart. In that moment, she knew that no matter what awaited her at the magical academy, she had the love and support of her family, and a sense of humor to guide her through any magical mischief that lay ahead.

Suddenly, Elara heard a gentle tapping at the front door, followed by the magical sound of tinkling bells.

"Your ride is here," her father said, pushing back his chair and standing.

Her mother stood, too. Her eyes were glossy with tears. "Already?" Together, the three of them crossed through the house to the front door.

Elara opened the front door to find a magnificent floating carriage drawn by two shimmering winged unicorns that glowed in the early morning light waiting outside, and she gasped at the sight. She knew it would be invisible to mundanes and only magical folks like herself could see it. Her gaze followed the length of the carriage. She followed the intricate details etched onto each window, and was awe inspired when she spotted the sparkling glass roof.

As she watched in amazement as they teleported her luggage to the top of the coach and strapped to the roof by unseen hands. After a heartfelt and teary-eyed goodbye with her parents, Elara was finally ready to go. Or at least as ready as she ever would be. A small step slid out for her to use. Elara felt a small push at her back, though no one but her parents were there. With the urging, she stepped up and into the carriage, settling onto the luxurious velvet seat.

With a rush of wind, the carriage lifted off the ground and glided through the air toward its destination, the Charmcaster Academy. Elara tried to look outside, but the unicorns were running through the cloud cover, leaving nothing to stare at. With every new mile they passed, excitement welled up inside Elara until she felt like she was practically bursting with anticipation for what lay ahead at her new magical school.

CHAPTER TWO

O rion Evergreen inhaled deeply, savoring the lush, earthy scents that enveloped the plant nursery. The air was thick with the earthy aroma of fresh soil, intermingled with the fragrance of blooming flowers. To Orion, it was a botanical wonderland, bursting with vibrant colors and diverse flora. Bright daisies dotted the scene, their cheery faces adding pops of yellow and white. Roses flaunted their blossoms in a dazzling display of pinks and reds, while ferns stretched out their leafy fronds, creating a cool, green canopy overhead.

Orion felt a light breeze caress his skin before it fluttered through to wave the ferns. The soft chirping of birds as they flitted from branch to branch was followed by the occasional buzz of a bee or a fluttering butterfly looking for a soft place to land.

On his knees beside a small table, Orion's slender fingers fluttering over a fern that was more slump than fronds. Yet, with each gentle wave of his hand, his magic helped the fern stir to life, straightening it's leaves as if trying to high-five the sunlight pouring in from the glass ceiling above.

"Orion?" his mother called softly as she stepped into the nursery with an envelope in her hand. "A letter arrived for you, honey."

A wide smile lit up Mrs. Rhonda Evergreen's face as she located her son, Orion, tucked away amidst a jungle of bustling plants, his dark brown skin sporting a dewy glow from the exertion and humidity. He wore his usual attire, a long-sleeved sweatshirt, grass-stained jeans, and worn-out high-tops. Orion turned down his mother's offer to buy him new kicks anytime, but he loved this pair and that was that.

With his curly black hair forming a halo around his square-shaped face, Orion leaned closer to a wilting fern, his expression focused and empathic.

He gave the fern an encouraging smile, his voice gentle yet firm. "Hey there, little one. I know you've been struggling. The climate here is a bit different from your native soil. But you're stronger than you think."

Orion's fingers traced over the fern's withering fronds, his tone turning more serious and his magic swirling around him. "We all have to adapt sometimes, and I believe you can, too. I'll help you, but I need you to help yourself as well. Can you do that for me?"

His dark eyes were filled with warmth and empathy as he coaxed the little fern, a testament to the unique bond he shared with the green patients under his care.

"Orion?"

He lifted his head and peered at his mom over the rim of his black-framed glasses, his expression transforming from surprise to a bashful grin, the signature look of a shy, fourteen-year-old plant whisperer.

"Here," she said, holding out the envelope. "This came for you."

Orion hesitated for a moment before standing and taking it from her. He held the envelope cautiously, not opening it, but tracing the edge of the seal with his thumb. A nagging fear tugged at his heart. What if the letter was a rejection? As much as he wanted to learn more about his own magic, part of him hoped it was a refusal. At least then, he wouldn't have to leave the safety of his home or his beloved plants.

His mother noticed his hesitation and gave him a gentle nudge with her arm. She was a pretty African American woman with a round face, her brown skin glowing under the greenhouse's sunlight. Her hazel eyes were warm and kind, and she wore a grin so earnest it could've sprouted seeds. Orion noticed she knotted her hair into a messy bun, as she smoothed out a wrinkle in her light blue dress and matching sandals.

"Go on, open it," she urged, her voice soft and encouraging.

"Mom," he whispered, his expressive brown eyes filled with worry. "What if the academy doesn't want me?"

"Nonsense," she said firmly, placing a comforting hand on his shoulder. "You have a gift for plant manipulation. You're meant to be there. And no matter what happens, we're proud of you."

"I-I don't know if I should go..." Orion stammered. "What if I'm not accepted into the academy?"

"Orion, you'll never know unless you open it," his mother said gently, her face full of compassion and understanding.

Taking a deep breath, Orion tore the envelope open, unleashing the magical missive held within. His hands shook as he unfolded the crisp parchment, scanning the letter quickly. He stared at the words. He reread them twice, then a slow smile crept across his face.

As the realization dawned on him, they had actually accepted him to Charmcaster Academy of Magic and Elements. His heart started trembling with slight trepidation and nervous jitters churned in his stomach.

"Mom... I got in," he said, his voice hoarse with emotion.

"Of course you did, honey," she replied, hugging him, then stepping back. "I always knew you would. There was never any doubt!"

Orion held the letter, still not entirely convinced that this was real. He had always dreamed of attending Charmcaster Academy, but now that the opportunity was here, he couldn't help feeling a pang of fear. He wanted to make his family proud, but what if he wasn't brave or strong enough to succeed?

"But Mom...do you really think I'm up for this?" Orion asked, his eyes wide and brimming with doubts as they skimmed over the glossy surface of the letter. "I mean, I've never been away from home before."

"Of course, you're ready," she responded with a swift nod, her gaze never wavering from his. "You may not see it yet, but I know you're braver and stronger than you think. You were born with green thumbs and a heart full of magic, Orion. The academy is lucky to have you."

"But what if I don't fit in?" His voice wavered, trepidation clear in his tone.

His mother's reassuring smile didn't falter. "Oh, honey, you'll find your roots. You'll bloom and grow, just like these plants around us. You just have to trust yourself and remember that being different is what makes you special." As he looked into his mother's warm, hazel eyes, Orion saw the radiant pride and unwavering love reflecting at him. "Plus, every first year is going to feel the exact same way as you do right now. And all of you will do just fine. You'll see."

Orion inhaled the rich scent of earth and plants that filled the greenhouse, his fingers tightening around the crumpled letter pressed against his chest. "Mom, I'm kinda torn here," he admitted, his words stumbling out in a hushed tone. "Part of me wants to dive into this adventure, but another part is freaking out. I'm scared, but... I want to make you proud."

His mother pulled him into a tight embrace, her own voice filled with emotion. "Oh, Orion, you've already made us so proud. We believe in you, always. Don't let fear, or anything else, hold you back."

With goofy grins on their faces, Orion's father, James Evergreen, and his grandmother, Nana Evelyn, entered the plant nursery.

"We heard Orion received mail today." His father exuded confidence and warmth, sporting a stylish chambray shirt with botanical prints, dark denim jeans, and worn in leather boots. "Well, son, is it true? Did you get an acceptance letter?" his father asked, clapping his son on the shoulder.

"Yeah, Dad," Orion said, holding up the letter. "I start classes tomorrow."

His father beamed. "I always knew you had the magic touch, son."

The sun's rays filtered through the glass ceiling above, casting a warm glow on the array of potted plants and vines that filled the room.

"Yes, yes, we've been believers all along," Nana Evelyn interjected, her silver curls twinkling beneath the radiant sunlight. She exuded elegance, sporting a vibrant maxi dress adorned with flowers, complemented by her beaded necklace and intricate earrings. "You should feel blessed, Orion, to have this opportunity to attend such a prominent school."

"Thanks, Dad. Thanks, Nana." Orion's voice creaked with the words. His fingers nervously played with the edge of the acceptance letter.

"Son, you don't seem as excited as we thought you'd be," his father said, concern etched on his face. "What's bothering you?"

"Uh, well," Orion hesitated, looking down at the floor. "I'm not sure I'm ready for this, you know? It's a big change, and I don't want to disappoint everyone."

Nana Evelyn placed a gentle hand on his arm. "My dear boy, you mustn't worry about disappointing us. We love you no matter what, and this is a great opportunity for you to learn more about your magic. You're tougher than you think, Orion."

"Your Nana's right," his father agreed. "It's natural to feel nervous, but we wouldn't encourage you to go if we didn't believe in you. You have a talent, Orion, and Charmcaster Academy is the perfect place to hone your gifts."

As they spoke, Orion noted the sincere expressions on their faces. He realized that his family truly believed in him, and perhaps he needed to believe in himself, too. That all of this was a lot of effort to waste on some kid who Charmcaster Academy didn't find worthy.

"Okay," he said, swallowing the lump in his throat. "I'll give it my best shot. I don't want to let you all down." He reached to touch the petals of a daisy, "And that means you too. I'll come back even better, I promise."

"Trust me, you could never let us down," his mother reassured him. "We're always here for you, honey."

"Besides, Orion," Nana Evelyn said with a wink, "you might find that the world of magic is bigger and more fascinating than you ever could've imagined."

"True. Who knows, Nana," Orion replied, adjusting his glasses with a smirk. "Maybe I'll even discover a secret spell for summoning pizza whenever I want. That would be some cool magic."

Nana Evelyn laughed, her laughter echoing through the greenhouse. "Oh, Orion, always thinking with your stomach! Well, if you find that pizza spell, make sure to share it with your dear old Nana. I could use a magical slice or two myself!" She drew him into a big hug. He rested his chin on her head. He started doing that when he had the last growth spurt, making him taller than Nana.

Everyone laughed. Hearing them cheer him on, Orion felt something stir within him, something that felt a lot like anticipation. This magical boarding school thing? Maybe he could rock it after all. His family was his very own pep squad. Their encouraging words were a rush to his ego, firing him up, pushing back the shadow of a doubt that had been trying to sneak in. With his folks in his corner, he felt this baffling mix of nerves and excitement. Like he was about to jump off a cliff and into the biggest adventure of his life.

"All right, I'll go," Orion said with a nod.

His family cheered and embraced him, their excitement contagious. But deep inside, his anxiety still bubbled under the surface. Orion's thoughts drifted to what lay ahead. He wanted to master his plant manipulation abilities, but fear clung to him like thorny vines.

In that moment, the fern Orion had been fussing over earlier suddenly went into overdrive like it had just downed an energy drink. Its fronds shot up like a rocket, reaching for the ceiling and intertwining with neighboring plants as if they were old friends having a wild dance party. Orion had to laugh—it was like the fern was mimicking his own bundle of nerves and excitement.

"Huh," Orion muttered to the rebellious fern, "well, a little green friend seems like you've got more personality than I gave you credit for."

"Whoa there, son!" His father chuckled, his eyes widening at the sight of the rapidly growing fern. "I guess the green thumb gene runs in the family, huh?"

Orion let out a nervous laugh, trying to steady his racing heart. "Yeah, I guess so, Dad. Who knew I could turn a wilting fern into a wild jungle adventure?"

"Well, dear boy, at least now you won't have trouble finding your way through the school's botanical gardens. Just follow the trail of runaway plants!" Nana Evelyn grinned.

Orion smiled at his grandmother's playful remark.

With a deep breath, he focused his energy, willing the fern to settle down. "Thanks for the advice, Nana. I'll try to keep my powers in check. No more plant parties without permission, right?"

"Right," his mother chided. "But occasionally it might be fun."

He closed his eyes and took a deep, steadying breath. As he exhaled, he felt the fern respond, its growth slowing down and returning to a more manageable pace. He opened his eyes to see his family watching him with understanding and love.

"Guess I still have a lot to learn," Orion admitted sheepishly.

"That's what Charmcaster Academy is for, honey," his mother said. "Now, go pack your things before the carriage arrives."

"Carriage?" Orion asked.

His family smiled and laughed.

"The best way to travel," his father said. "Now let's hurry, son. It should be here very soon."

Orion and his father left the plant nursery and strode up to their farmhouse, which stood proudly on the same acre of land. Orion's home was a rustic structure with peeling white paint and dark green shutters. Easy enough to fix, but no one seemed worried enough to paint it. The two ascended the creaky porch steps to enter the three-story house, the scent of familiarity enveloping them. Orion's bedroom was in the attic, on the third floor, and the two of them made their way up the narrow staircase.

His bedroom door stood ajar, and they entered the large, yet odd, shaped space. They painted the walls in a lively shade of forest green, as if bringing the outdoors in. In one corner of the room, a small collection of potted plants thrived under Orion's care. The lush and thriving pothos plants sit vibrant and content on a shelf, their cascading vines trailing gracefully toward the floor. Beside it, it perched a mischievous Venus flytrap with its jaws agape, eagerly awaiting the next unsuspecting insect to come along. And showcased on a wooden shelf was Orion's prized possession —Seymore. The stubbly green cactus sat perfectly upright, his spiky arms reaching toward the sky.

His father cast a look at the Venus flytrap. "You know, son, with powers like yours, you might want to keep an eye on that flytrap. We wouldn't want it snacking on any unsuspecting visitors."

Orion grinned, imagining the mischievous plant in action. "Don't worry, Dad. I'll make sure it sticks to flies and keeps its leafy appetite in check."

His father stepped over to a wall, where a makeshift door created a storage closet. He hauled out two large suitcases and dragged them closer to Orion's bed. "Only pack what you need for school, okay?"

"Okay, Dad. I'll use my magic to pack. If that's okay?"

His father nodded. "Go for it."

"Carry me off?" Orion wrinkled his nose and pushed up his glasses, waiting for his dad's answer.

"You'll see," Dad said, and Orion knew better than to ask for clarification.

"Carry me off?"

With a flick of his wrist and a whispered incantation, Orion tapped into his plant magic. The leaves of his plants fluttered in the air, similar to a maestro waving his wand before his symphony. He guided his clothes and books into the open suitcases, neatly arranging them with a touch of magical finesse. Then he took Seymore, the cactus plant, and carefully cradled him in his hands, gently situating his long spikes between the layers of clothes for safekeeping. "It won't be long and will get you out for some fresh air, I promise."

Outside the open window, a gentle breeze rustled the leaves on the oak trees near the house as a soft humming sound filled the air. The source of the noise revealed itself in the form of a magnificent flying carriage drawn by two winged unicorns. Their coats shimmered like opals under the warm sun, while their wings stretched wide.

"No way!" Orion said, unable to tear his eyes away from the magical sight. "That is so cool."

"Your chariot awaits," his father said with an encouraging smile. "I have always wanted to say that."

"Sure, Dad." Dragging the suitcases downstairs, Orion and his father met his mother and grandma in the living room. "I thought I would have more time. Even with magic, I still ran out of time."

"Well, honey, it is time now." Mother tipped her head back and said something Orion couldn't make out. "Okay, time for goodbyes," his mother announced, wiping away the tears that formed in her eyes. "We don't want Orion to miss his ride to Charm-caster Academy."

One by one, Orion's family hugged him tightly, their emotions raw and genuine. But he sensed they were holding back some. As he was, too. He shouldn't be scared. He was doing this.

Tears streamed down his mother's cheeks as she whispered, "I'm so happy for you, my brave boy. You're going to do amazing things."

"Make sure to stay in touch." His father's voice cracked as he pulled Orion into a tight hug. "We want to hear all about the crazy magic stuff happening at that new school of yours."

"Yeah, Dad, I promise," Orion replied, his voice trembling slightly. His own eyes welled up with tears, mirroring the emotions swirling inside him.

"And don't forget," Nana Evelyn added, "we're always here for you. No matter where you are, you'll never be alone."

Amidst the bittersweet farewells, Orion reluctantly stepped away from the warm embrace of his family, his heart heavy yet filled with anticipation for what lay ahead. Taking one last look at their familiar faces that radiated love and pride, he mustered the courage to walk out the front door, ready to dive headfirst into the unknown depths of Charmcaster Academy.

He knew it wouldn't be all smooth sailing. A lot can happen—and go wrong—in four years. But with his family by his side, Orion felt a fire light up inside him. He was ready to tackle whatever came his way, driven by the love and support that surrounded him.

Standing in the open doorway, Orion took a deep breath, the nervous energy within him somewhat dissolving.

"No turning back now," Orion whispered to himself, gripping the handle of his worn suitcases tightly. His family, right behind him, walked outside with him to see him get carried away to his new adventure.

The magical carriage drawn by two magnificent winged unicorns hovered near the front door of their home. All he had to do was get in it to be whisked away to the island of Mythos Isle, where the Charmcaster Academy awaited.

"Take care, honey," his mother said, giving him a reassuring nod. Again.

"You too, Mom," Orion said, swallowing hard as he approached the carriage.

With those parting words, his two suitcases were removed from Orion's grasp as if by unseen hands and the luggage floated upward, settling and strapping themselves to the top of the carriage.

As he climbed aboard, Orion hesitated for a moment, glancing back at his family once more. Was he really doing this? Could he really do this? For four years?

"Go on, son," his father urged. "We'll be right here waiting for you when you return for the winter break."

With a final nod, Orion settled into the soft cushions. The door closed behind him with a soft click, muffling the sounds of his family's last round of farewells.

As the unicorns flapped their majestic wings,

Orion felt the carriage lift off the ground. His stomach churned with a mix of excitement and anxiety.

"Goodbye!" Orion shouted out the window, watching as his family grew smaller below him.

"I love you, honey!" his mother called back, her voice barely audible over the wind. "Safe travels."

"Write often!" his father added, waving at his son.

As the Evergreen homestead disappeared from view, Orion turned his gaze toward the horizon as it slipped away. "I can do this," he said.

As the flying carriage zoomed toward Mythos Isle, secretly and invisibly located in the heart of the Bermuda Triangle, Orion's heart raced like a turbocharged broomstick. Within minutes, the carriage approached the lush island.

All of his studies, all the stories he was told, hadn't prepared him for seeing it in person. The view through the crystalline windows was straight-up, jaw-dropping gorgeous. Mythos Isle spread out below him like a mind-blowing scene from a fantasy movie, split down the middle by the three canals called the River of Reveries. He leaned out the window and spotted Lumina Woods, its tall trees all lit up with the infamous glow-in-the-dark moss.

A whole forest of mythical creatures and

enchanted plants? It was like stepping into a make-believe world!

On the north side, Orion glimpsed Starfall Meadow with its insane celestial light show. The field was sparkling, like a chunk of the night sky had crash-landed right there and he knew that the flowers only bloomed under starlight, reflecting the constellations above. As he flew over the middle of the island, Orion gasped as a gigantic colosseum, like a superhero arena, came into view.

Moments later, the carriage touched down in front of Charmcaster Academy, perched on a hill like it owned the place. Orion thought the enormous castle was an impressive sight, with its spires and towers reaching majestically to the sky, while the stained-glass windows threw colorful patterns of light onto the grounds. A massive courtyard was situated in the center of the property, surrounded by lush gardens and sprawling lawns.

Orion opened the carriage door and wondered what adventures awaited him in this next chapter of his magical life.

CHAPTER THREE

E lara's heart raced as she stepped into the Great
Hall of Charmcaster Academy. She knew this
room was where students had their meals,
received important announcements, celebrated holi-
days, and often socialized.

Elara's eyes popped wide open, and her breath
hitched at the sight of the cavernous hall stretching out
in front of her. The sky-high ceiling, crowned in a riot
of twirling, twisting banners, seemed to pulse in tune
with her heartbeat. Sculptures of legendary Charmcasters adorned alcoves in the ancient stone walls, and a
few became animated. The lifelike figures leaning out
of their gilded nooks and waving their hands at the
fresh-faced students. One motherly looking statue even
blew a kiss as Elara went by.

Elara moved further into the room and could feel the air crackling with magic all around her. Tables sprawled across the hall. All carved with the symbols of the distinct elements: a dancing flame for fire, a graceful ripple for water, a rustling leaf for earth, a whistling gust for wind, and a twinkling crystal for ether. *Oh, and the chairs!* They were ornately carved and draped in a riot of vibrant colors, and the massive chandeliers dangling from the rafters bathed the hall in an ethereal glow. Above her, a ceiling that mimicked a starry night sky twinkled with constellations. Looking up, Elara almost bumped into two fellow students that were also looking up at the constellations. Both pointing out their birth sign when they found it. Though she wanted to look closer too, Elara knew there would be more time for that later. It was all so much to take in at once. Too much for even one day. Just the fact that she arrived in a flying carriage was a lot for Elara to take in. She could hardly believe her eyes. And this was going to be her home for the next four years!

At the far end of the vast space, a grand stage supported an elevated table and a podium, where she recognized Headmistress Nightshade, standing with an air of authority that demanded respect.

"Welcome to Charmcaster Academy," said a

woman near the entrance, her voice warm and inviting. Her dark hair cascaded down her back, a contrast against her royal-blue robes that swirled around her gracefully as she moved. "I am Professor Rosalind Mistral, your Weather Magic instructor."

"Hello, ma'am. Nice to meet you," Elara replied. "I'm Elara."

"Enchanted to meet you, young Elara."

Professor Mistral welcomed another student, and Elara stepped aside.

Taking a deep breath, Elara approached one of the long tables, draped in an opulent fabric of gold and purple. As she took her seat, she found herself flanked by a diverse assortment of her fellow students.

"Hey there." Elara turned to see a boy with dark skin and black-framed glasses. She guessed he was probably fourteen or fifteen. He smiled and gestured at his clothing with interesting plant motifs. "Orion Evergreen, plant whisperer," he said in a quiet, almost shy voice.

"Elara Silverwind. I'm a friend of the wind," she replied with a smile, feeling an instant connection with her classmate.

"Hello!" From across the table, a tall girl with pale skin and blonde hair, her attire adorned with celestial shapes, smiled widely at her. "Greetings! I'm Aria

Moonlight, and I have a knack for manipulating moonbeams." Her flowy attire featured soft pastels and lunar patterns.

"Flint Rockwell." A stout young man with pale skin, messy dark hair, and practical, earth-toned clothing sat beside Aria. His square face seemed to match his gruff voice. "And I'm all about the Earth."

"Hello, everyone! I'm Ivy Whispersong." A petite girl with startling green hair and emerald eyes spoke up next, her clothing patterned with leaves and flowers. "I can talk to plants. And they talk back!" She giggled. Elara noticed the plant whispering boy smiled from ear to ear with Ivy's introduction.

"Name's Cyrus Stormbringer." A tall, lean boy with a stormy expression introduced himself next, his clothing embroidered with silver lightning bolts. "I conjure storms and command lightning." As if to show off, a lightning bolt flashed above his head, then faded. Everyone let out a collective gasp in awe.

Finally, a girl with warm hazel colored skin and raven-black hair gave a dismissive wave. "Whatever. I'm Zara Pyre." Her bold red and orange clothing was loose and flowing like flames. With a graceful motion, she raised her hand and unfurled her palm, conjuring a delicate flame that flickered and danced, casting a red radiance upon her skin. "So yeah, I play with fire." Zara fisted her hand and doused the spark.

As they finished their introductions, Elara marveled at the array of magical abilities among her new peers. She felt a surge of awe and excitement bubbling up inside her, fueled by the thought of what she could accomplish alongside them. Every fiber of Elara's being was set on fitting in, finding her place, and mastering her own magic abilities while at Charmcaster Academy. Nothing would deter her from pursuing her goals, and she embarked on her journey with unwavering passion and resolve. And a bit of a queasy stomach from all the adrenaline.

Elara glanced up at the platform as Headmistress Nightshade stepped forward to address the new students from the podium. The tall, stately woman with olive skin and jet-black hair wore elegant robes in dark-purple hues. Her commanding presence instantly captured the attention of everyone in the Great Hall.

"Welcome, first-year students, to Charmcaster Academy. I'm Headmistress Nightshade," said the imposing woman, her voice resonating throughout the room. "We have chosen you to join our ranks because of your unique magical abilities and potential for greatness."

Elara grinned, her heart thumping in anticipation.

She eagerly listened to the headmistress's words, making Elara even more excited about the fresh start of the school year.

"Throughout this year, our esteemed faculty will guide you, learning not only how to hone your individual magical skills but also how to work together as a team," continued the headmistress. "Charmcaster Acadcmy aims to foster a sense of unity among its students, as we believe that our combined strengths will enable us to create a brighter future for us all."

As the headmistress's voice boomed through the Great Hall, Elara's gaze darted around the room, taking in the animated faces of her fellow students. It filled the room with a magical buzz, as if every student had swallowed a jar of enchanted fireflies.

"Your magical education will be demanding, and there may be times when you feel overwhelmed or disheartened," warned Headmistress Nightshade. "But remember, those who share your passion and desire to succeed surround you."

Elara nodded, mentally preparing herself for any challenges that lay ahead. She knew that her course at Charmcaster Academy wouldn't be easy, but she resolved to excel and make the most of this incredible opportunity.

Looking up, she smiled at the translucent apparitions of little dragons that soared gracefully through the air, their vibrant forms shimmering with otherworldly beauty, before playfully darting out of the windows like mischievous little escape artists.

"Now," Headmistress Nightshade said, raising her hands as if to cast a spell, "it is time for you to receive your first-year school uniforms."

Suddenly, the air in the Great Hall shimmered with magic, and piles of neatly folded clothes appeared before each student. Elara gasped in delight as she beheld the Charmcaster Academy uniform for girls: a black vest, a plaid purple and black skirt, a crisp white short-sleeved shirt, knee-high socks, and sturdy black boots.

"Wow," Elara whispered as she grabbed the uniform floating in front of her. It felt like a tangible symbol of her newfound identity as a Charmcaster, and she couldn't wait to wear it.

The other students grasped their hovering uniforms with broad smiles. Mumbles of conversations floating about, Elara hearing words such as, "cute" or "look at mine."

"Before we dismiss you to your dorms, I want to remind you that while we fill Charmcaster Academy with wonder, there are also many mysteries and dangers lurking outside these walls," Headmistress

Nightshade said, her voice taking on a slightly ominous tone. "Stay vigilant and do not enter the forests or leave the grounds of the academy without an adult escort."

The headmistress's words sent a shiver of unease down Elara's spine, like a ghostly finger tracing icy trails down her back. She cast a quick glance at her fellow students, finding mirrored expressions of apprehension.

"Welcome once again to Charmcaster Academy. May we fill this year with growth, discovery, and magical memories."

Cheers and applause filled the Great Hall.

Elara's eyes flickered to Professor Mistral, who was engrossed in an intense conversation with another teacher, their features obscured by a mysterious hooded cloak. Their heads were close together, their lips moving in silent conversation. Professor Mistral's earlier calm demeanor was replaced with an expression of deep concern, and the very air surrounding them crackled with a shadowy energy.

A knot of unease twisted in Elara's gut. What could have them so rattled?

Elara couldn't hear what they were saying, but the palpable tension radiating from them indicated that something was terribly wrong. But what? With a final conferring whisper, both figures stepped through a secret panel in the wall that opened and shut without so much as a sound. Just like that they were gone.

Assuming it was a debate about school business, Elara returned her attention to her uniform. Her heart swelled with pride as she touched the academy emblem sewn into the fabric. She looked around the Great Hall, taking in the enchanted banners, the living statues, and the array of students.

"Can you believe we're here?" Elara's eyes widened with wonder as she turned to Orion. "This place is absolutely incredible!"

"Yeah, it's... it's kind of surreal," he replied, his smile faint but genuine.

Elara beamed, clutching her new uniform against her chest. "I can't wait to dive into wind magic. There's so much I want to learn! What about you? What are you most excited about?"

Orion nodded. "I'm looking forward to mastering my plant manipulation magic."

Glancing around at their fellow tablemates, Elara couldn't contain her excitement. "Everyone here seems so talented. I can already tell we're going to learn a ton from each other."

Orion absentmindedly adjusted his glasses. "Yeah, I

guess." His gaze shifted to the uniform in his hands, and he grew quiet.

Aria leaned closer, her voice filled with concern. "Did you hear what Headmistress Nightshade said about needing a chaperone to leave the grounds?"

Ivy furrowed her brow, looking uneasy. "Yeah, it gave me the chills. What do you think she meant?"

Elara shrugged, her voice uncertain. "I'm not sure. Maybe it's just a safety measure, so we don't get lost on the island."

Orion nervously fidgeted with his sleeve. "Or... there could be dangerous creatures lurking outside the academy's walls."

"Don't worry," Elara reassured him, sensing his unease. "We're here to learn magic and make friends, remember? We won't venture beyond the castle grounds."

"Yeah," Orion agreed, taking a deep breath. "Let's be cautious. Who knows what's out there, including students from the other two academies."

Aria grinned mischievously, leaning closer to Orion. "Maybe there's a secret dragon lair out there, and they only let the bravest students find it! How cool would that be?"

Ivy rolled her eyes, then snickered. "Yeah, and I bet the dragons throw the best parties, too."

Elara snorted with a grin. "You two are crazy. A dragon party would definitely burn down the house."

Everyone softly laughed. A corny comeback, but funny.

"Attention, first-year students!" a stern voice rang out. It was Headmistress Nightshade, standing at the head of their table. "It's time to head to your dorms and get settled in. Tomorrow will be a busy day filled with classes and orientation activities." She whirled about, then halted and spun back around. "Remember what I told you. No one is to leave the school grounds without permission from me or one of my delegates."

Elara frowned. Why was Headmistress Nightshade so adamant about this? Before she could ask questions, however, Nightshade had already turned on her heel and left without another word.

The students rose from their seats.

As Elara joined the flow of students exiting the Great Hall, a chill tickled her spine, making her wonder if the castle had a secret stash of ice cream or if it was something more sinister. Shadows danced playfully in the corners, as if they were hiding their own mischievous plans. She hugged her uniform closer, hoping its magical fabric had the power to ward off the eerie vibes.

Orion walked beside her along the corridor. An

occasional flutter of wings or the soft padding of paws echoed through the hallways. The air smelled strangely sweet, like a mix of exotic flowers and spices.

Elara noticed her new friend's breathing was shallow and that he had a death grip hold on his uniform.

She placed a hand on his shoulder and gave Orion a reassuring smile. "It's okay," she said softly. "We'll be in our dorms soon and nothing can hurt us inside the academy."

Orion only nodded and kept his eyes trained ahead of him. They filled the twisting corridor with a soft, unearthly light, casting a surreal and dreamlike hue over the walls. They lined the floor with luminous stones, and along the walls, Elara saw strange symbols and runes that seemed to pulse and vibrate with an ancient power. The ceiling shimmered with blinking planets and shooting stars.

"Wow, those stars on the ceiling are cool, aren't they?" Elara said as she glanced upward.

"Yeah," Orion replied, his gaze following hers. "It's like the night sky, but indoors. Kind of comforting."

Elara nodded. "A bit like how you probably feel around plants, I bet."

His eyes lit up at the mention of flora. "Oh, yes!"

he exclaimed. "There's something about being surrounded by green that's just so peaceful."

"I bet." Elara was looking forward to learning more about her new friend and his plant magic.

Shrugging off her own unease as just exhaustion from a long day of traveling, Elara continued down the hallway in silence.

CHAPTER FOUR

Orion gave Elara a hesitant smile before parting ways in the dimly lit hallway. He took a deep breath and entered the castle wing reserved for the first-year boys' dorm rooms. The stone walls seemed to close around him, as the cold, sheen-like marble flooring beneath his feet echoed with the sound of footsteps and laughter.

He clutched his uniform tightly as a familiar wave of anxiety washed over him. Meeting new people had always been a nerve-racking experience for Orion, as he often found solace and comfort in the company of plants rather than other humans. But he was here now and there was no turning back. His father's words came back to him, *"You are stronger than you think."*

Flickering torches cast brilliant iridescent light

along the corridor, illuminating the portraits of esteemed Charmcaster professors that lined the walls. Just like the statues in the Great Hall, their watchful eyes followed his every step, curiosity gleaming in their painted gazes.

As Orion ambled down the corridor, the tapestry on the wall beside him suddenly stirred. Materializing from the woven threads was a mischievous green elf, its enormous eyes glinting with impish charm. Before Orion could react, the creature deftly snatched the uniform from his hands, giving him a cheeky grin.

"Don't worry, Orion Evergreen!" the elf squeaked in a voice as small as himself, already scampering away with the uniform clutched in his tiny hands. "I am happy to take your uniform straight to your room for you!"

With a flicker of magic, the elf and the uniform vanished into thin air, leaving a dumbfounded Orion standing in the now empty corridor before he could even interject.

This place is certainly weird, he thought.

As Orion continued walking, the temperature in the hall dropped. A sudden frosty breeze swept past him, causing him to shudder involuntarily.

"Lost, are you?" a ghostly voice whispered.

Orion jumped back. Before him floated an ethereal

male figure, its translucent body shimmering like moonlight on water. It had no face, but Orion could sense its friendliness.

"Um, no. Just heading to my dorm room," Orion replied, trying to maintain eye contact with the faceless specter.

"Ah, very well then," the ghost responded, its voice echoing softly. "Good luck, young Charmcaster." With a wave of its transparent hand, the apparition vanished into thin air, leaving Orion feeling slightly more unnerved than before.

Orion shook off his unease from his hallway encounters and finally entered the wing of the boys' dorms, peering into the rooms as he passed them. Open doors revealed glimpses of the other students practicing magic within their rooms. In one bedroom, a boy with sandy hair and an aura of concentration that defied the laws of gravity, was levitating various objects with a mere flick of his wrist. The books, a crystal ball, and playing cards, all suspended in mid-air, traced a whimsical tango under the young Charmcaster's command.

Across the corridor, another boy stood at the center of the room, his intense gaze focused on the water-filled orb in his hands. With a wave of his hand, the water inside swirled and formed miniature cyclones, a testament to his skill in hydromancy.

Orion couldn't help blurting out, "Whoa, dude! That's some next-level water bending."

The boy turned toward Orion with a grin, water droplets glistening in his spiky hair. "Thanks, man! I've been practicing my water-bending techniques since I was a guppy. Wanna see something really cool?" He extended his palm, and a water snake slithered out of the orb, playfully splashing water in Orion's direction. "Careful, though. Don't want to get soaked on your first day!"

Orion laughed, raising his hands in mock defense. "No worries, I've got my raincoat ready! Show me what else you got, water wizard!"

The boy's eyes lit up with mischief as he conjured up a waterspout that danced and twirled above their heads. "Prepare to be amazed!"

"So cool," Orion said and moved along.

Further down, Orion glimpsed a duo engaged in a friendly competition of telekinetic chess. The game pieces moved of their own accord, responding to the invisible push and pull of the players' psychic commands. The chessboard was like a cool battlefield of wits and magic, a spectacle that left Orion in awe.

He paused to glance into a room, the walls painted

with celestial symbols, where a lean boy with spiky white hair sat in a circle of soft, magical sunlight. He was manipulating the sunbeams to cast intricate shadow plays on the wall, each figure moving with life-like precision under his manipulation.

Each door offered a peek into a world Orion was about to become a part of. It stirred a sense of over-whelming wonder within him. "This place is like a magical theme park, and I've got a golden ticket."

Orion continued toward his room and smiled when he saw friendly tiny creatures of light, known as lumisprites, flitting through the rooms. One of the lumisprites hovered near him, its shimmering wings brushing against his cheek before darting away friskily. He chuckled and said, "Hey there, little buddy! Mind showing me the way to my room? I'm still figuring out the magical GPS around here."

The lumisprite chirped as if understanding and zipped ahead, guiding Orion to his destination.

When he found his room, Orion was relieved, but hesitated in the doorway, his hand gripping the metal handle of the partially open door. He wrestled with his doubts and fears, struggling to dispel the anxiety that threatened to consume him from being so far from home. His mother said, *"You're going to do amazing things."* And exhale.

He pushed the door wider, and Orion's eyes settled on the bed nearest to the door, where his luggage sat neatly stacked. He could see his favorite coat spilling out from the suitcase, a reminder of the home he left earlier in the day. So many changes, so fast. His head was spinning. With a deep breath, he took a tentative step inside, feeling the weight of the new world he was entering.

Orion mentally recited his motivations for coming to Charmcaster Academy. He wanted to summon his courage, to make his family proud, and, most importantly, to prove to himself that he possessed an inner strength far greater than he ever realized.

His thoughts drifted back to his family, their encouraging words echoing in his ears. They believed in him, and he couldn't let them down. "*You're going to do amazing things.*"

"All right, Orion," he muttered to himself. "You can do this. You belong here. They invited you here. They want you here."

But the thought of sharing a room with a stranger —a fellow Charmcaster—made him feel vulnerable and exposed. Back home, Orion had attended public school, but he made no real friends and he had always felt distant and alone. If asked, he said Seymore was his best friend. He would just leave out the cactus part.

What if his roommate didn't like him? What if they didn't get along?

"You got this," he whispered. "You can't let fear hold you back. Be brave."

With a determined nod, Orion stepped further inside. He took in the two simple wooden beds on opposite sides of the room. The scent of freshly laundered linens mingled with the faint aroma of old oak that wafted from the polished floorboards. The faint smell of fresh paint still lingered, too. Opposite of him was the other bed, which was neatly made up and waiting for its occupant.

Who would he be? What abilities would he possess?

As if in answer to his questions, the door creaked open behind him, revealing a stout and muscular young man with dark hair. "Hey, plant dude!"

Startled, Orion saw a boy standing at the threshold, a crooked grin plastered on his face. Then Orion remembered seeing him at the welcome orientation in the Great Hall only a few minutes ago.

"It's me, Flint Rockwell," the boy said, extending a dirt-specked hand. He was well built, with a fair complexion, a strong jawline, and thick locks of ebony hair. His earth-toned clothes blended into his tanned complexion, making him look like a living embodiment of the very element he wielded. "You must be my new roommate." With an effortless gesture, Flint demonstrated his powers by creating a small mound of soil in his palm.

Orion swallowed before responding. "Orion Evergreen," he replied, shaking Flint's hand hesitantly. "Nice to meet you... again."

"Same." Flint chuckled. "So, what do you think of our humble abode?"

"Um, it's comfy, I guess," Orion replied, glancing around the room once more.

"Sure is," Flint replied with a grin, stepping over to his own bed. He seemed completely at ease with the situation, as if sharing a room with someone new was no big deal at all.

"Have you been here long?" Orion asked, trying to ignore his uneasy thoughts.

"Arrived pretty early morning," Flint said, unpacking his own luggage. "I've heard great things about this academy. Can't wait to start learning some real magic."

"Me too," Orion agreed. "But from what I see, it looks like you are already pretty good at it."

"There's always something new to learn."

As they continued unpacking, Orion's mind swirled with doubts and insecurities. Would he be able to live up to the expectations placed upon him? Could he truly belong in a place like Charmcaster Academy?

"You don't mind having a roommate?" Orion asked.

Flint folded up a wrinkled T-shirt. "Nah. I've heard the academy can get pretty intense, so it's good to have someone to talk to. Plus, it'll be fun learning about each other's powers. You're into plants, right?"

"Uh, yeah," Orion admitted. "I can manipulate flora and fauna. But it's not as cool as your earth powers, though."

"Hey, don't sell yourself short," Flint said, tossing the shirt into a dresser drawer. "We both have unique abilities, and that's what makes us special. Besides, I bet you'll be a tremendous help in the academy's gardens. Plants need soil and dirt, right?"

Orion grinned, appreciating Flint's kind words. "Sure, I guess we all need each other's magic to make ours work. I just hope I can keep up with all the other Charmcasters here."

"Trust me, we're all learning together," Flint said. "And as roommates, we've got each other's backs, right?"

"Right," Orion agreed, feeling some of his uneasiness fade away.

He knew he had a long journey ahead of him here

at Charmcaster Academy, but with friends like Flint and Elara by his side, perhaps it wouldn't be as scary as he'd initially thought.

"Hey, that girl you were with earlier, Elara, right? Is she your girlfriend?"

"What?—*no!*" Orion sputtered, his cheeks burning like stove burners. "We just met today, and I already consider her a friend. There's just something about her that seems friendly. Nice, ya know?"

"Ah, gotcha," Flint replied, nodding in understanding. "Yeah, she seems cool. You two will make a good team."

Orion changed the subject to something less mortifying than girl talk. "So, I've read there's some scary creatures living on the island."

Flint's eyes lit up, and he leaned in closer, as if eager to share the tales he'd heard. "They say the forest is full of all sorts of mysterious beasts. Some can even lure you deeper into the woods."

"Really? That's creepy." Orion's heart raced as he imagined coming face-to-face with one of those creatures, unsure if it was friend or foe.

"Yep," Flint said, grinning. "And bro, that's not even the worst of it. There are these massive spiders with venom so potent it can put you in a coma for weeks. And then there are these bear monsters—"

"Wait, what's so bad about bears?" Orion interrupted, curious. "I mean, they're just regular animals, right?"

Flint shook his head, his expression somber. "Not these creatures. Their growls can send shivers down your spine. It's said that if you face off with them, you're as good as dead."

Orion gulped at the thought of such terrifying animals lurking just beyond the academy walls. He knew there'd be odd challenges during his time at Charmcaster Academy, but he hadn't anticipated quite so many literal monsters.

"Wow," he said, frowning. "That sounds next level scary."

"Definitely," Flint agreed, his voice low and serious. "But don't worry too much about it. They say the forest is off-limits to students unless accompanied by a teacher or on a special assignment. So, as long as we don't go wandering in there alone, we should be fine."

"Good to know," Orion said, trying to push away the frightening images that were now firmly lodged in his mind. But then he had the thought of the beasts getting out of the woods and into the doors. Great, now he's scared of what ifs and what's real.

As they continued unpacking and settling in, Orion felt a little more at ease with Flint as his roommate. Though his uncertainties still lingered, the prospect of navigating school with real friends made everything seem slightly less daunting. And perhaps, just maybe, he could prove to himself and others that he was already braver and stronger than he was just yesterday.

Orion and Flint had barely finished unpacking when a sudden scream echoed through the hallways, followed by an eruption of laughter. The boys exchanged wide-eyed glances before dashing out of their room and down the corridor.

As they rounded a corner, they stumbled into the main study hall, a grand chamber adorned with high bookshelves, wooden tables, and plush armchairs. A warm glow emanated from enchanted lanterns that floated near the shelves, casting intricate patterns of light across the floor.

"Quick! Someone do something!" A boy cried out.

Orion's gaze was drawn to the windows, where the curtains had caught fire, causing students to scramble in panic. Amid the chaos stood a red-haired boy, his hands raised defensively as he chuckled uneasily.

"Stand back!" shouted a tall boy, thrusting his arms forward. Water gushed from his palms, extinguishing the flames before they could spread.

The room fell silent as everyone stared at the now

drenched and charred curtains. It was a stark reminder of the power these young Charmcaster students wielded, and the potential risks that came with it.

"What happened?" Orion asked. "That kid could've burned down the school!"

"Relax," Flint said, placing a hand on Orion's shoulder. "Looks like someone was just showing off."

Orion followed Flint's gaze to the sheepish-looking boy with bright red hair standing next to the window, where the curtains were now smoldering. The boy's fingers still emitted faint wisps of smoke, indicating that he was the one practicing fire magic.

"Classic Matt," another kid said, shaking his head. "Always trying to impress everyone with his dumb fire tricks."

"Hey!" the redheaded boy named Matt protested, crossing his arms. "I didn't mean for it to get out of control."

"Next time, just try not to set the school on fire, all right?" Flint said, a hint of amusement in his tone.

A round of relieved laughter filled the room, dissipating the tension. Orion glanced over at Flint, who shook his head.

"Uh, well," Matt stammered. "I guess I need to work on my discipline a bit more."

"Guess there's never a dull moment around here," Flint commented, grinning.

"Definitely seems that way," Orion agreed.

The incident had served as a vivid reminder of the challenges and responsibilities that came with being a student at Charmcaster Academy.

"Come on," Flint said, clapping Orion on the shoulder. "Let's retreat to our glorious abode and bask in the overwhelming joy of unpacking socks and arranging our toothbrushes. Thrilling stuff, I tell you."

Orion wondered what his own role would be in this new chapter of his life. As much as Orion wanted to prove his bravery and make his family proud, his heart still raced with anxiety whenever he thought about the unknown challenges that lay ahead. And to make his nerves worse, he now needed to worry about fires getting out if hand.

CHAPTER FIVE

When she parted ways with Orion, Elara treaded into a long hallway that led to the first-year girl's dorms. Her heart fluttered as she clutched her uniform close to her chest. They lined the hallway with gleaming golden sconces that gave off a soft, flickering light across the weathered stone walls. It was unlike anything she had ever witnessed before, like an intriguing mix of old-fashioned architecture and ethereal charm.

As she walked down the hall, a flock of miniature shimmering butterflies darted through the air overhead, their wings catching the light as they weaved in and out of the chandeliers. Then a pair of enchanted tapestries came to life, depicting scenes of powerful witches and elemental creatures locked in fierce battles.

Watching the battles play out like a movie, Elara said, her eyes wide. "Wow! This place is so awesome!"

Elara bounced on her toes, a bubble of excitement welling up in her chest as she skipped down the hallway. Zillions of questions zipped around in her mind like hyperactive dragonflies.

How was she going to tame her wild wind magic? What new friends would she make? Would she have to share her secret stash of candy?

Elara turned a corner and nearly bumped into three girls who had just emerged from an adjacent corridor. Among them, she recognized the familiar faces of Aria Moonlight, Ivy Whispersong, and Zara Pyre. Her three classmates were also clutching their newly acquired school uniforms, their excited chatter filling the air.

"Hey, Elara!" Aria called out, her voice like a silver bell. She flashed a radiant smile at Elara. The girl stood tall and willowy, with skin as white and smooth as porcelain. Her heart-shaped face, framed by an angelic halo of golden locks, cascaded down to her waist in tumbling waves. "Fancy meeting you here. Do you want to walk to the dorms with us?"

Elara instantly liked the girl with the calming voice. "Sure!"

The four girls fell into step together, their footsteps

echoing through the ancient hallway as they continued toward the first-year girl's dormitory.

"Isn't this place incredible?" Ivy asked, her green eyes reflecting the flickering light. "It's so much more than I ever imagined." She added.

Elara noted that Ivy stood no taller than five feet, with an angular face and sharp jawline, softened by bright green hair that hung in a bob to her shoulders. Her clothes featured botanical prints in shades of emerald, and she wore a long necklace with a delicate leaf pendant.

"Definitely," Zara said, her voice filled with excitement. The girl's eyes glowed with the same fire as the braziers that lit up the corridor. She was curvy, with warm-toned skin and a round face with dark hair flowing around her. "I can't wait to see our dorm rooms!"

"Where are you all from?" Aria inquired, her gaze drifting over the others with genuine interest.

"I'm from the Windy Glades," Elara replied, her thoughts drifting back to the swirling gusts of air that seemed to dance around her childhood home. "Wind magic seems to come naturally to me."

"Ah, that's why your hair always looks like it's caught in a breeze!" Ivy teased gently, the corners of her mouth curving into a playful grin. "I'm from

Verdant Grove, myself. Plants and I have always had a special connection."

"Me too!" Zara exclaimed, her dark eyes sparking with enthusiasm. "Well, not plants—I have a way with fire. I'm from the Flame Valley, where the volcanoes never sleep."

Aria nodded thoughtfully. "I come from the Lunar Island," she shared, her voice soft and melodic. "My magic is tied to the moon and its phases."

"You all have such amazing abilities," Elara said, feeling a newfound sense of camaraderie with her fellow students.

As the girls continued to exchange stories and share their excitement about the upcoming school year, the ancient walls around them seemed to absorb their words, welcoming them into the legacy of Charmcaster history.

Just as the girls rounded a corner, a sudden whirlwind of colors caught their attention. Three elves, each a different shade of green, dashed out from the shadows. They appeared small and mischievous, their bright purple eyes twinkling in the hallway's light. They wore simple clothing in deep blue, rimmed in purples, and on their heads were small pointy hats. The elves moved lighting fast, snatching the neatly folded uniforms from the girls' hands before anyone could protest.

"Hey!" Elara exclaimed, her eyes wide with surprise.

"Your uniforms," one elf said, "we take them to your rooms."

Another elf said, "No worry, young Charmcasters, we'll have them nice and tidy for you!"

As swiftly as they had appeared, the magical creatures vanished down the corridor, leaving the girls exchanging bewildered glances.

"Charmcaster Academy's one wild rollercoaster, huh?" Ivy chuckled, her green hair shaking with her laughter.

"Totally," Aria said with a giggle. "Can't wait to see what wacky thing pops up next."

A curious Elara added, "It's only day one."

"Oh! Speaking of surprises," Zara said, pointing toward an ornately carved door at the end of the hallway, "I think we've found the girl's study hall."

Elara pushed open the heavy oak door, stepping into a vast room filled with the soft chatter of students and the hum of magic at work. The study hall was breathtaking—high ceilings adorned with shimmering crystal chandeliers, walls lined with towering bookshelves, and plush velvet chairs scattered throughout the space. Warm sunlight filtered through the stained-glass windows, casting kaleidoscopic patterns onto the polished wooden floor.

Elara's eyes sparkled with awe as she observed her fellow Charmcaster students showcasing their supernatural skills. A girl, her locks as blue as a cloudless sky, twirled her hands, conjuring a mini whirlpool right in her palms, making water dance and swirl like it had a mind of its own. Not to be outdone, another student, her hair a fiery tapestry of autumn leaves, commanded a cluster of stones to defy gravity, floating in mid-air as if they were the ultimate levitating rock stars.

The air pulsed with energy, and Elara could feel the familiar tingling sensation of her own dormant wind magic longing to be unleashed. She glanced over at Aria, who seemed equally enchanted by the spectacle before them.

"Isn't this amazing?" Elara whispered, her eyes wide with wonder.

Aria nodded, her light gray colored eyes reflecting the vibrant display of magic before them. "It's incredible to see so many talented Charmcaster students in one place. I don't feel like I need to hide myself away."

"Think of all the things we'll learn," Ivy said, her excitement palpable.

"Exactly," Zara agreed, grinning. "We're going to

become powerful Charmcasters. I just know it! Maybe the best this school has ever seen."

Elara felt a newfound sense of purpose stirring within her to not only master her wind magic abilities, but to also carve out her own place in this magical world.

They continued across the room toward the three jutting corridors that Elara thought must lead to their actual dorm rooms that were probably more epic than secret chambers guarded by dragons.

"Isn't it beautiful here?" Elara asked Aria.

"It truly is," Aria replied, her eyes sparkling like the crystals above them. "I've seen nothing quite like it. I have read some books with magic in them, but I never thought it would look so cool in real life."

Ivy and Zara waved goodbye and disappeared down the corridor on the right, leaving Elara and Aria feeling a tad lost. The two girls exchanged uncertain glances, their brows furrowed with confusion.

"Do you know which way to go?" Elara asked.

Aria shook her blonde head. "No... not really."

Just as Elara was about to suggest flipping a coin to decide, a cat-like creature popped out from behind a suit of armor. It had tiny wings and fluffy, rainbow colored striped fur. The creature hopped onto Aria's shoulder, its voice a curious mix of a purr and a chirp. "Need a hand, gurrrls? Or a paw, purrrhaps?"

Elara giggled and nodded. "Yes, please. We're trying to find our dorm room. Could you, um, maybe help us out?"

The cat gave a playful flick of its bushy tail. "Of course, dear Charmcasters! I'm Minx, your durrrm room guide extraordinaire. Just follow meow lead!"

With that, Minx took off, fluttering through the air like a fluffy missile. Elara and Aria exchanged amazed looks before chasing after the whimsical creature.

Minx led them through the corridor, then turned to the left.

"This way, ladies!" Minx called over his shoulder, as they turned a corner into a hallway that glowed with a soft, enchanting light.

As they neared the end of the hallway, the cat stopped next to a closed door. "Here we are, gurrrls. Many blessings to you both."

Aria smiled. "Thanks, Minx! You're a true dorm room wizard."

Minx purred contentedly, his wings flapping with pride. "Just doing my job. Enjoy your magical journey." And with that, Minx fluttered away.

"Ah, here we are. Room nine hundred and eighty-one." Aria gestured toward the door with an ornately carved bronze plaque bearing the number.

"We're roommates!" Elara exclaimed, her heart racing with delight. "This is going to be an amazing year. I can feel it."

Aria smiled warmly. "Me too."

As they entered their dorm room, Elara felt a strong sense of belonging. She knew that this was where she was meant to be, and she couldn't wait to fully embrace her life as an academy student.

The walls of their shared room were painted a lustrous rose gold, and the room was illuminated by two wall-mounted sconces, their golden reaching every corner. Two four-poster beds adorned with thick velvet bedspreads stood against opposite walls. Each was graced with a lush collection of silken pillows in shades of cream and gold.

"Wow," Aria gushed, taking it all in. "This is so much better than I imagined."

"Isn't it incredible?" Elara agreed, sitting down on one of the beds. "It's like something out of a dream. I thought it would be like a hospital room or something else bland and colorless. But this? This is beautiful."

Elara noticed they made the curtains around the beds out of a sheer, gauzy material that shimmered.

She reached out to touch them, marveling at their ethereal quality.

Her eyes sparkled with delight, as she couldn't contain the bubbling excitement inside. "Wow, everything looks so pretty," she gushed, her voice brimming with enthusiasm. "I can't believe we're really here, Aria!"

Aria's face lit up with awe as she nodded in agreement. "Totally! I've been dreaming about this place forever, but actually being here feels even more magical."

Elara noticed her Charmcaster uniform neatly folded at the foot of the bed, as the elves had promised. Her heart swelled when she thought of herself wearing it, finally being a part of the magical world she had always longed to join.

"I can't wait to put on our uniforms tomorrow," Elara said.

Aria grinned. "We'll finally be officially Charmcasters."

Their eyes met, and they shared a moment of understanding. The girls went about unpacking their belongings and chatting about their lives.

When they finished, Aria and Elara returned to the Great Hall for a late lunch. Elara had thought only an hour or two had passed, but time seemed to behave differently within the academy, with clocks occasionally speeding up or slowing down, making it an unpredictable realm where moments could stretch or vanish in a blink.

As Elara ate her sandwich and munched on her salty fries, she thought about the diverse range of students she had met so far. Each one possessed unique magical abilities, and she felt a growing sense of purpose to fit in among them.

"I'm going to become a wind magic master," she whispered.

Aria took a sip of her soda and raised an eyebrow. "Elara? Are you talking to yourself?"

Elara blushed slightly. "Oh, sorry! I was just reminding myself of my goal. There's just so much to be amazed about here. I've never seen such a variety of people and magical skills before."

Aria scanned the room. "You're so right. Charmcaster Academy is like a magical melting pot of awesomeness!" Aria nodded enthusiastically, a smile spreading across her face. "We're on this magical adventure together, Elara. It's going to be epic!"

A massive grandfather clock bonged out the hour, stating it was past nine o'clock in the evening and everyone in the room yawned, even Elara. Weird because Elara had thought it was only lunchtime. Could it be night already?

"Let's go back to our room." Aria said with droopy eyes. "I'm suddenly tired and we have a big day tomorrow."

The girls shuffled back to their dorm room and changed into their nightgowns.

"Goodnight, Aria," Elara said softly, standing near her bed.

"Goodnight, Elara," Aria replied, the moonlight streaming through the window casting a silvery glow on her face as she climbed into her bed. "Sweet dreams, roomie."

The room seemed to hum with a quiet energy, as if the very walls were whispering secrets of magic yet undiscovered. And though she had only just arrived, she could already feel herself being drawn deeper into the enchanting world of Charmcaster Academy.

As Elara got ready to turn in for the night, she noticed something strange about her bedpost. It was etched with intricate symbols she had never seen before. She traced them with a finger, and suddenly, an eerie glow filled the room. The symbols started shifting, forming a sentence she could read: "*Beware of the Shadows' Grasp.*"

As the words dissolved, an icy shiver touched her

skin. She did not know what it meant. She glanced over at Aria, but her roommate seemed to be fast asleep, unaware of what had just happened.

"Aria? Did you see that?"

Her roommate pulled the blankets over her head. "No, Mom. I'm sleeping," she mumbled.

She got into bed, but sleep didn't come easily for Elara. A chilling wind blew through the dormitory window, rustling the curtains like whispers from an unseen presence. The shadows seemed to move closer, encroaching upon the edges of Elara's bed. But even as she tried to shake off her fears, the nagging unease refused to leave her. It clung to her like a cold mist, wrapping itself around her thoughts and seeping into her heart.

Whatever the message meant, it wasn't anything good.

"Nothing will harm us here," Elara murmured, snuggling under the warm blankets. "We're safe at Charmcaster Academy."

As sleep finally claimed her, she vowed to discover the meaning behind the mysterious message.

CHAPTER SIX

O rion fidgeted with the collar of his new Charmcaster Academy uniform as he waited for Elara in the corridor that led to the classrooms. His roommate, Flint, had darted off to raid a magical vending machine that spit out troll-shaped gummy snacks. The fabric of his uniform felt stiff and slightly scratchy against his skin, a constant reminder that he was no longer at home, but in an entirely new and intimidating world. He was sure he'd learn faster if he could wear his baggy jeans and hoodie.

"Hey, Orion!" Elara's voice echoed down the hallway as she hurried toward him. "How are you finding the uniform? I think it's rather stylish, don't you?"

"Uh, yeah," Orion answered, forcing a smile. "It's

just taking some getting used to, I guess."

Orion's jacket was a rich royal purple, complementing a white button-down shirt and a striped tie boasting the same regal purple and the style rounded off with sleek black slacks. Elara grinned alongside him in her own uniform: a snug black knit vest over a cute short-sleeved shirt, her own necktie boasting the same colors as Orion's. A mini-skirt of plaid purple and black hugged her legs above her knee-high black socks and glossy, patent-leather Mary Jane shoes.

They began walking toward the classroom together, Orion's eyes darting nervously around the hallways as he tried to remember which way they were supposed to go. Elara, on the other hand, moved with purpose, her excitement for the day ahead evident in every step.

"Isn't this place amazing?" she gushed. "I can't believe we're actually here, learning about all these incredible forms of magic. I've been dying to get my hands on some weather spells ever since I found out about my affinity for wind."

"Y-yeah, it's definitely... different," Orion replied, trying not to let his anxiety show too much.

"Come on, there must be some type of magic that's got you geeking out. What's your jam?"

"Plants, I guess." The nostalgic memories of his

family's nursery filled his mind. "I used to spend hours in my family's nursery back home, experimenting with growing and shaping plants. But honestly, I'm just hoping to not totally embarrass myself. I am still working on the control part."

Grinning, Elara gave him a friendly shove. "You're gonna kill it, Orion. You just gotta trust yourself a bit more, buddy."

Orion mustered a small smile. "Thanks, Elara."

They walked in silence and as they passed the open door of a classroom, they paused to peer inside. The Potions Classroom contained cauldrons that seemed to have a mind of their own. They bubbled and brewed concoctions and occasionally released puffs of colored smoke that formed into playful shapes or whispered cryptic hints about upcoming exams.

Continuing toward their own classroom, Orion glanced at his new friend.

"Flint's my roommate," he said. "He seems nice enough, but we're so different. He's all about Earth manipulation and seems really tough. I hope we get along."

"Just give it some time, Orion. As for me, I'm rooming with Aria. She's super sweet. Plus, a plant guy and an earth guy learning from each other makes perfect sense."

"True. If I was rooming with a fire Charmcaster, I would be worried about my little green friends." Orion felt a little more at ease when they arrived at the classroom door, though his nerves still fluttered beneath the surface.

It was an expansive room and soft gusts of wind blowing around them, carrying the scent of fresh rain and the distant rumble of thunder. All of it was as if a storm had brewed within the walls. The ceiling was a beautiful display of a clear sky with fluffy white clouds that moved slowly, casting shadows on the desks below.

"By the grace of the four winds." Elara whispered, her eyes ballooning as they soaked in the grandeur of the over-the-top classroom. "This is mind-blowing!"

Orion bobbed his head, his jitters forgotten in the face of such awe-inspiring surroundings. "It's like we've stepped into the great outdoors, but... we're indoors?"

"I know!" Elara threw her hands up dramatically, like she'd just won a trip to Disneyland.

Orion hesitated for a moment before settling into the seat next to Elara. His brown eyes stared at the tide of students swarming in.

"You doing, okay?" Elara asked, noticing his furrowed brow.

"Y-yeah," Orion replied, forcing a smile. "Just taking it all in, I guess."

"Fair enough," she said, giving his shoulder a friendly tap. "Hang tight, Orion. This is going to be an epic experience."

The classroom seemed to be bubbling over with the eager buzz of students psyched for the start of their first Weather Magic and Mystical Artifacts class. Orion spotted among the students Aria Moonlight, Ivy Whispersong, Cyrus Stormbringer, Zara Pyre, and his roommate, Flint Rockwell. It was nice to see familiar faces.

Suddenly, the classroom began to hum with supernatural activity. The wind outside picked up, causing the leaves of the trees outside the windows to rustle and sway. The clouds in the ceiling shifted, casting eerie shadows across the floor.

"Attention, class!" A smooth, confident voice called out, silencing all the chatter in an instant. The professor strode into the room, her royal-blue robes flowing gracefully around her. She swept her dark hair up in a loose bun, tendrils framing her warm, gentle face. She exuded an air of tranquility, and the entire room seemed to settle under her presence.

"Welcome to Weather Magic and Mystical Artifacts," she said, her voice as soothing as rainfall on a tin roof. "I am Professor Rosalind Mistral, and it will be my pleasure to guide you through the fascinating world of atmospheric manipulation." She gestured toward the stormy ceiling, which responded to her movements by changing the color of the sky to a brilliant sunset.

"Nice," murmured Ivy, leaning forward in her seat, her green eyes alight with delight.

Zara seemed equally entranced, while Flint simply nodded appreciatively.

"Today, we'll be focusing on the basic principles of weather magic," Professor Mistral continued, clasping her hands together. "Mastering this art lies in awareness of the balance between the elements that make up our world: air, water, earth, and fire. When these forces are in harmony, we can create a vast array of weather phenomena."

Orion swallowed nervously, his hand instinctively reaching for the small plant in his pocket. He can control plants with ease, but the idea of manipulating the very elements themselves was daunting.

"Excuse me, Professor?" Cyrus raised his hand, his stormy-gray eyes curious. "How do we begin to learn such powerful magic?"

"I'm glad you asked that, Cyrus," Professor Mistral replied. "We'll start by studying the different techniques and spells that Charmcasters have developed over the centuries. Once you have a solid foundation, we'll move on to practical applications. One step at a time. The order in which you learn is very important. Remember that when you think you have a bright idea."

As she spoke, the classroom continued to come alive with magical energy. The wind howled outside, wrapping the room in a cocoon of sound, while the clouds above shifted and morphed into various shapes, such as animals, people, even entire landscapes, before dissolving into wisps of mist.

"Remember," Professor Mistral said gently, as if sensing Orion's anxiety, "the art of weather magic is not about wielding power, but in understanding it. This journey will be one of discovery, growth, and ultimately, mastery."

As the class progressed, Orion became more and more captivated by the subject, despite his initial unease. The world of weather magic was vast and mysterious, full of untapped potential and incredible possibilities. And with Professor Mistral's guidance, he believed that maybe, just maybe, he could find his place at the academy. "*You're tougher than you think.*"

"Today, we will embark on a journey of recognizing the forces that shape our world, the winds that cool our skin, the rain that nourishes life, and the storms that test our resolve," Professor Mistral announced, her eyes gleaming. "Over this term, we will explore the history of weather magic, learn about its various branches, and delve into the techniques that have been passed down through generations of Charmcasters," she continued. She paced around the room in her flowing robes, leaving a trail of mist behind her as she spoke to her pupils. "From the gentlest zephyr to the fiercest tempest, we shall unlock the secrets hidden within the elements themselves."

"Are we going to learn how to summon tornadoes?" Flint asked, his voice gruff.

"In due time, Flint," Professor Mistral replied with a nod. "But first, we must begin with the basics. The most fundamental lesson in weather magic is learning how to sense and channel the energies that flow around us. The first spell we will practice is the Nimbus Charm, which allows us to summon a small cloud and manipulate its properties."

Everyone stood up and waited for instruction.

"Focus your energy on the tip of your finger, and envision the cloud you wish to create," she instructed, demonstrating the technique flawlessly, as a tiny, puffy cloud appeared above her head. "Now, repeat after me: 'Nubifuror.'"

"Nu-bi-fu-ror," the students mimicked, their fingers held high and steady. Some managed to produce wisps of vapor, while others struggled to summon anything at all.

"Good effort, everyone," Professor Mistral spouted words of encouragement. "Weather magic is as much about your connection to the elements as it is about the words and hand movements."

As the students practiced, Orion felt a growing sense of frustration as he failed to produce even a hint of a cloud. He focused his energy on his hand, repeating the incantation over and over, but to no avail.

"Orion, you seem to have some trouble," Professor Mistral said, her voice gentle. "Take a deep breath and clear your mind. Weather magic requires a calm and centered approach."

Taking her advice, Orion inhaled deeply and exhaled, releasing his tension. As he tried again, this time with a newfound sense of serenity, a small puff of vapor appeared above his head.

"I did it!" he exclaimed.

"Excellent progress, Orion." Professor Mistral praised him, her smile warm.

As the class continued, they learned how to control

the size and shape of their clouds, as well as the manipulation of raindrops and snowflakes.

"Our next lesson involves more advanced techniques, such as summoning lightning and controlling the temperature. Anyone with a wind or storm ability will excel at this power," Professor Mistral explained. "But for now, I want you all to practice what you've learned today. It is an art that takes time and patience to master."

"Professor Mistral," Ivy said, "can we combine our abilities? Like, if I were to work with someone who can control water, could we create a beautiful rainstorm together?"

"That's a great question, Ivy," Professor Mistral replied, her eyes sparkling with enthusiasm. "Yes, of course. Combining your abilities with those of your classmates can yield some truly awe-inspiring effects. However, it requires a deep understanding of one another's magic and precise coordination."

"Does that mean we could potentially create a tornado?" Flint asked, his fingers tapping on the table, as if he was imagining the earth rising up within a powerful whirlwind.

"Creating a tornado would be a dangerous endeavor, Flint," Professor Mistral cautioned. "But if you were to collaborate with someone like Cyrus, who has storm manipulation abilities, you could achieve a similar effect on a smaller, safer scale. Charmcaster Academy is all about learning to harness your powers responsibly."

"All right, class," Professor Mistral announced, clapping her hands together. "Now that we've touched upon the basics of Weather Magic, let's move on to a fascinating discussion of mystical artifacts." She moved to the front of the room and stood behind a podium. "Artifacts are supernatural objects that have been imbued with powerful enchantments. They can be both helpful and dangerous, depending on who wields them and for what purpose."

"Can artifacts enhance our abilities?" Elara inquired.

"In some circumstances, yes they can," the professor replied, gripping the sides of the podium. "For example, the Amulet of Storms, which can amplify a storm manipulator's powers, should be used with extreme caution."

As the students listened intently to Professor Mistral's words, Orion found himself wondering what kind of artifact might aid his plant manipulation abilities. He imagined vines growing rapidly at his command, and for once, he didn't feel anxious about it. Instead, he felt a sense of excitement and hope.

"Next week, we will delve deeper into the history and properties of specific artifacts," Professor Mistral continued. "And who knows? Perhaps someday, you may even have the opportunity to wield one yourself. Now, before we conclude today's class," Professor Mistral said, her voice taking on a somber tone, "I would like to discuss a particular artifact known as Aegis of the Ancients. A group of powerful sorcerers created it. But it is quite hazardous, for it has the power to dissolve the protective barrier around Mythos Isle, exposing our magical world to mundane humans, which would cause all sorts of untold chaos."

"Professor," Ivy said, her voice wavering slightly, "Why would anyone create such a dangerous artifact?"

Professor Mistral nodded. "The sorcerers who crafted this relic meant for it to be a last resort, a failsafe device, should our world ever face an insurmountable threat. However, they underestimated the corrupting power of such a relic."

As Professor Mistral spoke, Orion's hands clenched into fists, and he found himself holding his breath. He glanced over at Elara, who seemed more fascinated than frightened.

"Has anyone ever tried to use Aegis of the Ancients?" Flint asked, his gruff voice betraying a hint of concern.

"Thankfully, no one has wielded its powers thus far," the professor replied, though her expression remained grave. "But there have been attempts throughout history, and many have sought to harness its destructive capabilities for their own gain. The artifact is now under the protection of the Charmcaster Academy, where we strive to ensure that it never falls into the wrong hands."

"Isn't it risky to keep something like that here?" Zara asked.

"Not really. The academy is one of the few places capable of containing and safeguarding such a formidable artifact," Professor Mistral assured them. "Aegis of the Ancients is locked away in our most secure vault, protected by powerful wards and enchantments. We have had no incidents involving the relic since we placed it under our protection."

Despite her words, Orion could feel his anxiety mounting. He knew he should trust the professor's expertise, but the thought of such a dangerous artifact at the school was unsettling. Worse than what lurks in the woods.

"Let this be a lesson to all of you," Professor Mistral warned, her eyes scanning the room. "Magic is an incredible gift, but it also has the potential for great destruction. It is our responsibility to use our powers wisely and protect the delicate balance between our world and the human realm."

As the conversation continued, Orion felt his unease grow like twisted vines, constricting his chest and making it difficult to breathe. He glanced over at Flint, who seemed unbothered, his stony face betraying no emotion. Orion envied his roommate's calm exterior.

"That is all for today, young Charmcasters. You all did well and I'm proud of your efforts," Professor Mistral called out as the students filed out of the classroom. "I'll see you all next week."

As the students dispersed, Orion and Elara lingered behind, and Professor Mistral approached them.

"Orion, Elara," she said, her voice soft but steady. "You both have shown a great aptitude for magic, and I can see that you're eager to learn more. If you're willing, I would like to give you a tour of the artifact vault after lunch. There's extra credit in it for you both."

Elara grinned. "That would be great, Professor."

"Yeah, I mean yes, ma'am," Orion said. "I'm interested."

"Excellent," Professor Mistral smiled. "Meet me there after you've had your meal."

As they made their way to the dining hall, Orion

noticed Elara's hands trembling as she wrung them together.

"What's wrong?" he asked.

"Something strange happened last night in my room," Elara said and moved to a quiet corner where they could talk privately. She told him about the bedpost glowing and emitting the cryptic message: '*Beware of the Shadows' Grasp.*'

"Maybe it's just some old Charmcaster legend," he said.

"No way. Those symbols are on my bedpost," Elara brought up. "They feel like a creepy '*Beware*' sign."

"It might just be your imagination messing with you, Elara," Orion said half-heartedly.

"No, I'm sure it was like a coded message or something," Elara insisted, her conviction unwavering. "I just wish I could crack it."

"We'll puzzle it out. We're Charmcasters, right?" Orion put on a brave front, even though his heart was thumping in his chest.

"True that, Orion," Elara responded, her gaze turning thoughtful. "This school does seem to have its fair share of hidden mysteries. I guess my bed is one of them."

CHAPTER SEVEN

After lunch, Elara and Orion made their way to the Charmcaster Academy's artifact vault.

The door opened slowly, revealing a dimly lit chamber, only lit by the soft glow of flickering torches. Elara and Orion stepped inside, and Elara's gaze roamed the room, taking in the various artifacts, some sparkling with a mysterious energy and others tucked away in darkness. The air felt still and heavy with the scent of old books and relics, along with a combination of musty papers and mysterious magics, hinting that powerful forces lingered here.

"This is really cool," Orion said, his voice echoing through the chamber.

Professor Mistral appeared from within and smiled at her two pupils. "Come with me."

She led Elara and Orion further into the room, her flowing royal-blue robes billowing behind her like clouds during a stormy day. As the professor of Weather Magic and Mystical Artifacts, Professor Mistral exuded a sense of calm authority that put Elara at ease, even in such a mysterious place.

"Today you will have the unique opportunity to learn about some of the most powerful and ancient artifacts in the magical world," Professor Mistral explained, as she gestured to the packed shelves. "But this is not a playground. We must treat these objects with the respect they deserve."

Elara nodded, feeling the weight of responsibility settle on her shoulders. She glanced over at Orion, who looked equally sobered by the professor's words.

"Of course, Professor," Orion said quietly, his eyes still scanning the room, no doubt wondering which artifact he would get to study first.

"Very well, let's begin," Professor Mistral said.

She led them through the vault, stopping occasionally to explain the history and uses of various items. Elara hung onto every word, her curiosity growing with each passing moment.

As they studied the artifacts, Elara noticed Orion's

fingers twitching slightly, as if eager to reach out and touch the ancient relics before them. She knew he felt the same pull she did, the allure of the unknown, the power and wisdom that these artifacts held within their ancient forms.

As much as they were eager to learn and explore, they also knew the importance of respecting the power that surrounded them. This was not a place for careless mistakes.

Professor Mistral guided Elara and Orion to a shelf holding an array of peculiar objects. The first artifact she pointed out was a small, ornate box adorned with intricate carvings and tiny holes.

"This," she said, "is the Wisp of Willows Box, used to contain magic that can grant temporary bursts of power when released."

"That's curious," Elara whispered, her eyes glued to the delicate engravings.

"Over here," Professor Mistral continued, gesturing to a twisted staff made from dark wood. "We have the Mighty Tempest, capable of summoning fierce storms." She paused, her eyes locked on the staff as if recalling a distant memory. "It belonged to a powerful Charmcaster who disappeared during a great battle, leaving the staff behind."

"Can it still summon storms?" Orion asked, pushing up his glasses with one finger.

"Absolutely, but only someone with a deep connection to the elements can unlock its true potential," Professor Mistral replied, her gaze lingered on the staff for a moment longer before moving along.

As they continued through the vault, the air grew thick with the weight of history and magic. Elara could feel the tension building within her, like a combination of adrenaline and trepidation coursing through her veins.

Professor Mistral pointed to a beautiful, dragon shaped pendant situated in a box of velvet fabric. She sighed softly. "The Dragon's Tear is believed to grant the wearer the ability to find true love. The gem at its center is said to be a tear shed by a dragon mourning the loss of its mate."

Before anyone could utter another word, a pulse of raw, untamed magic erupted from a small artifact resembling a golden orb, throwing out a shock wave that stirred the air like a summer squall. Elara instinctively clutched Orion's arm, her heart tap-dancing a fierce samba in her chest. Professor Mistral's eyes narrowed, a sliver of concern threading through her calm façade.

Elara and Orion were statues, eyes rounded with

nerves. The only un-moving thing was Professor Mistral as she advanced toward the cause of the disruption.

"Stay calm," she directed, her voice solid but carrying a subtle tone of alarm. "We've got ourselves a bit of an artifact power tantrum here. You know, sometimes these ancient treasures get a tad testy when they've been cooped up on a dusty old shelf for too long and the object needs to release a little magic."

Carefully, she reached into the orb's aura, her fingertips dancing with a cool blue light that seemed to pacify the pulsing artifact. The orb dimmed, retracting its aggressive aura until it was again a passive sphere. She placed it back on its velvet cushion.

With the magic tamed and everything back in its place, Professor Mistral turned to Elara and Orion once more. "So," she said breezily, "shall we continue our tour?"

Elara and Orion nodded, then trailed Professor Mistral toward the next curiosity.

As they delved deeper into the vault, Elara was caught between a sense of wonder and wariness over the raw power nestled in these artifacts, and yet comforted by Professor Mistral's grace under pressure. Which did not waver even with the lingering energy from the unexpected explosion still crackling in the air around them.

Professor Mistral's expression grew tense, her lips drawn into a thin line as she guided them to the next artifact. She tightly clasped her hands together, knuckles turning white from the pressure. The surrounding air seemed to grow colder, reflecting her unease.

"Professor Mistral," Elara began hesitantly, her voice wavering slightly as she tried to mask her own fear. "Is everything all right?"

Professor Mistral turned to face her, and though she attempted a reassuring smile, it failed to reach her eyes. "Of course, dear," she replied softly, but the edge in her voice betrayed her true feelings. "It's just... sometimes I worry about having these artifacts on school grounds, even though I know they are safe within the vault and I'm the only faculty member with a key and I keep it on me or locked away in my desk. Well, I still have some fear. These are ancient, magical artifacts and thus, highly unpredictable."

Elara nodded solemnly, and she felt the cool touch of her wind magic tingling at her fingertips, ready to spring forth if necessary.

Orion bent over to examine a small statue of a centaur. Elara didn't find it all that special.

"It is our duty as Charmcasters to respect and understand the potential dangers of these artifacts while also recognizing their importance in our magical world."

Elara swallowed hard, her throat suddenly feeling tight. "I understand."

"Let's continue," Professor Mistral urged, her voice firm but gentle. "There is still much to learn."

As they moved on, the room grew darker, filled with shadows that whispered of hidden dangers. She shivered, wrapping her arms around herself as if trying to ward off the chill that permeated the air.

I drew Elara into an imposing glass case containing a large, ancient trophy. It appeared to be forged from an unknown metal that absorbed and reflected light simultaneously. Shimmering gemstones bedazzled the front and Elara couldn't turn her eyes away.

"Is that...?" Elara trailed off, her breath caught in her throat as she stared at the awe-inspiring artifact.

"Ah, yes," Professor Mistral confirmed solemnly. "Aegis of the Ancients holds immense power, capable of shielding entire cities from harm or turning the tide of any battle, but such power comes at a cost."

"Cost?" Orion asked, his brow furrowing in concern. His glasses barely slid down the bridge of his nose, but he reflexively pushed them back up.

"Should Aegis of the Ancients fall into the wrong hands, the destruction brought forth would be catastrophic," Professor Mistral explained, her voice heavy with the weight of her words. "In the past, its misuse has brought entire empires to their knees. We must always remain vigilant, for the line between protection and destruction is perilously thin."

Elara shuddered at the thought. Its power was palpable, even through the glass barrier, and she imagined the devastation it could cause in malevolent hands.

"As the next generation of Charmcasters," Professor Mistral said, her voice taking on a somber tone, "it's important that you study these artifacts to understand their potential, both for good and ill will. One day, it will be your responsibility to ensure that they are used wisely, and not for selfish or destructive purposes."

"Professor," Elara hesitated, her voice thick with unease, "what's stopping these relics from ending up in the hands of some bad guy? I mean, if even one went rogue..."

Professor Mistral's gaze drifted over the rows of mysterious objects before settling back on Elara. Holding her palm up, "Stop. Don't worry. That will never happen on my watch," she said, her tone soft yet firm. "This vault is protected by numerous enchantments and safeguards. But ultimately, the responsibility lies with us, with our vigilance and understanding."

Elara hoped she wasn't out of line speaking up like she was, but she was genuinely curious. "So, does that make Charmcasters like you a magical gatekeeper?"

"To put it simply, yes, Elara, we are gatekeepers."

As they finally reached the end of their tour, Elara felt both relieved and strangely apprehensive.

"Thank you for showing us the vault, Professor," Orion said, his voice filled with gratitude. "This was amazingly insightful."

"Yes, thank you, Professor Mistral." Elara said as she glanced over her shoulder at the cases.

"Extra credit well earned," Professor Mistral replied, smiling.

They followed her out of the vault, the heavy door closing behind them with a resounding thud. As Elara and Orion made their way back through the corridors of the academy, Elara once again glanced back at the sealed entrance. A sense of foreboding settled over her like an icy blanket. Elara couldn't shake the feeling that something dark and dangerous stirred within the confines of the artifact vault... and it wouldn't stay hidden forever.

CHAPTER EIGHT

O rion stepped into the sunlit classroom, his eyes as big as saucers at the sight of the indoor jungle that made up the classroom for "Intro to Mystical Flora and Earth Magic: Communicating with the Green."

Walls disappeared behind a curtain of hanging ivy, the ceiling lost under a canopy of giant fern leaves that waved like friendly green clouds. Towering sunflowers stood like sunny sentinels, their faces following the dance of sunlight that played hide and seek across the room. Flowers burst out from corners, making the room look like a spilled rainbow. Creeping Virginia slithered across the wooden floor like slow-moving snakes, their leaves whispering secrets to one another.

A particularly bold shrub scuttled across the room on root-legs, as though late for an appointment.

Charmcaster Academy was many things, but dull was not one of them.

This wasn't just his favorite subject because of the chattering plants and the chance to flex his plant magic muscles. No, it was also because he was going to share this class with Ivy and Flint. Ivy, with her hair as green as the leaves they studied, and Flint, solid as the earth they connected with, were more than just classmates—they were his friends.

"Hey, Orion!" Ivy called out, waving him over to their usual table. Even at this distance, Orion could see her emerald eyes sparkling.

"Morning, guys," Orion said, taking a seat on a stool next to Ivy and Flint at the same lab table.

"All right, students," Professor Stonebrook said. The short man stood at the front of the class, dressed in earth-toned, business-like attire. If he wasn't in a classroom, Orion would place him as a zookeeper. He had Asian features, bronzed skin and dark-brown hair severely parted on one side. Either no one told him it looked ridiculous or he just didn't care. "Today, we'll be focusing on communicating with plants using your own unique magical abilities. Let's start by pairing up and practicing."

Orion could feel his heart rate quicken as he turned to Ivy, who was already grinning at him.

"Ready, partner?" she asked, her voice filled with enthusiasm.

"Let's try it," Orion said, trying to sound more confident than he felt. He was all too aware that his powers were still developing and unpredictable at times. And he definitely did not want to embarrass himself in front of Ivy.

"Students," Professor Stonebrook said, "you must form a connection through genuine understanding and empathy with all flora and Mother Nature herself. It's not about forcing the plants to do your bidding, but rather working in harmony with them."

Ivy nodded. Her eyes already closed as she reached out toward a small potted fern on the table. Orion watched in awe as the fern's leaves quivered and begin to sway gently, as if caught in a breeze, Ivy's telepathic connection guiding its movements. She opened her eyes. "This plant is thirsty."

"How do you know that?" Flint asked.

"Because of my uncanny ability to communicate with plants. Duh," she said, rolling her eyes.

"Whatever. Your turn, Orion," Flint said. "You've got this."

"Okay," Orion murmured, focusing on a tiny

sprout poking out from the soil in a nearby pot. He could feel the fragile life within it, its tender roots reaching down into the soil while its stem strained toward the sunlight above. "Grow," he whispered, as if he was telling it a secret.

But the sprout didn't just listen; it took his whisper as a challenge. It didn't grow—it zoomed! The plant rocketed skyward at a speed that would make a firework jealous. It's wriggly tendrils shot out, twisting and coiling around Orion's arm like a leafy anaconda.

"Um, help?" Orion stuttered, his voice threatening to squeak as the vine continued its exploratory wrap.

The classroom dissolved into stifled giggles and gasps. The normal order of growth turned topsy-turvy by a small sprout with big dreams. Something Orion could relate to.

"Stay calm, Orion," Professor Stonebrook called out, hurrying over. "Reign in your magical connection with the plant. Work together."

Orion took a deep breath, feeling the panic recede as he reminded himself of the professor's words. Reaching out once more, he gently used his magic to urge the plant to release its hold on him. Slowly, the vines unwound themselves from his arm before settling back onto the table.

"Good job, Orion," Ivy praised, smiling warmly at him. "You got it under control."

"Thanks," Orion said, relieved but still a little embarrassed by the mishap. At least Ivy didn't laugh like Flint did.

"Keep practicing, everyone," Professor Stonebrook instructed, giving Orion an approving nod before moving on to assist other students.

Despite the botanical screw up, Orion couldn't suppress his bubbling sense of achievement. Yeah, his powers were still a work in progress, but with Professor Stonebrook's mentorship and his buddies rallying around him, he felt like he was standing on the launchpad to magical awesomeness.

"You're going to do great things."

Orion's gaze involuntarily found Ivy. Watching her talk with plants was like seeing a star in its natural element; she sparkled, she beamed, she downright glowed. It stirred something in his chest, a fluttering that was as new and confusing as it was thrilling.

"That...that was embarrassing," Orion said to his friends. "My magic is a bit unstable."

"Oh, don't worry, Orion, we'll turn you into a legit plant charmer in no time," Ivy said with a sweet smile. "That is why we are all here, to get better at what we do."

"Legit plant charmer, huh?" Flint retorted, rolling his eyes. "Just make sure your unruly plants don't start bossing us around. I can already picture them demanding extra water and sunlight like divas. Or worse, the vines could trap us in our beds."

They all laughed. Orion thought Flint was funny and wished he had his confidence. Though he could seem a tad rude at times.

"Hey, do you think Professor Stonebrook will teach us how to talk to trees next?" Ivy asked, leaning over the table.

"Maybe," Orion responded. "That would be sick."

"Sure. Can't wait to spend my days talking to ferns and giving gardening tips," Flint quipped, rolling his eyes. "I want to do the cool, like out of this world stuff."

Ivy's radiant smile sent butterflies dancing in Orion's stomach. "Well, I've always wanted to have a chat with an oak tree. They're like wise old wizards, you know?"

Orion grinned at her, his attention utterly derailed. "That's how I feel about weeping willows. They are so beautiful and wise, like my Nana Evelyn."

Ivy, sitting right next to him, was doing some serious damage to his concentration. There was something about the way she'd barely run her fingers over the leaves, like she could read their stories. And when Flint tossed out his snarky one-liners, her laughter was like some spell itself—melodic and infectious. Man, this would not be easy. Too bad she wasn't like the girls back home who made his life easier by just ignoring him.

"Yo, Orion, you seem kinda spaced out," Flint remarked, quirking an eyebrow in his friend's direction.

"Oh, uh, yeah, I'm good. The plant thing has me kinda rattled, I guess," Orion blurted, attempting to brush off his daydreaming.

"If you say so, dude," Flint responded with a shrug.

The remainder of the class passed in a blur for Orion as he struggled to focus on his plant magic while simultaneously attempting to hide his new found crush on Ivy. He practiced his spell work diligently, but his thoughts never strayed far from her radiant smile and infectious laughter.

Just as Orion was finally feeling like he had gained some control over his emotions, a loudspeaker announcement echoed through the classroom, snapping everyone's attention to the box hanging from the ceiling.

"Attention all first-year students," a stern voice

boomed. "Please make your way to the Great Hall immediately for an important announcement."

The students exchanged puzzled glances, wondering what could be so important that it required their immediate presence. Professor Stonebrook looked equally surprised, but quickly regained his composure.

"All right, class," he said firmly. "It seems we have an unexpected interruption. Please gather your belongings and head straight to the Great Hall. We will continue our lessons tomorrow. Good work today."

The students shuffled out of the classroom. Orion joined the rest of their classmates in the corridor on their way to the Great Hall, uncertain of what awaited them there.

Cute little pixies zipped through the air, leaving trails of twinkling dust in their wake, their giggles echoing in the halls. Floating lanterns illuminated the way, their soft glow casting dazzling patterns on the walls. Even though it was daylight outside, the sun could never reach these long, twisty hallways.

Upon entering the Great Hall, Orion spotted Elara near the entrance, and made a beeline for her.

"Hey, Elara," Orion said, pausing beside her. "Any idea what's going on?"

Elara glanced at him. "Not a clue, but I'm curious. Let's get seats up front."

Orion, Ivy, and Flint followed Elara through the crowd as whispers of anticipation filled the air. They found seats at a long table near the podium on the platform. Headmistress Nightshade stood behind the lectern and on either side of her sat her fellow professors.

"Attention, students!" Headmistress Nightshade's authoritative voice boomed throughout the hall, instantly silencing the murmurs. She stood tall at the head of the room, her dark purple robes wafting around her. "We have gathered you here today to announce an event of great significance... the Otherworld Triad Tournament!"

"The what?" Orion whispered.

"Shhh," Ivy and Elara both whispered back.

A murmur rippled through the Great Hall.

Headmistress Nightshade cleared her throat. "Every year, the esteemed Otherworld Triad Tournament takes place, pitting Charmcaster Academy against our two rival schools: Fantasia School and Nebulous Institute." Her gaze swept across the room, her eyes flickering with a spark of intensity. "Each of these schools will put forth their six most talented first-year students, selected through a magical lottery," she continued, her voice steady and authoritative. "These chosen few will compete in a variety of magical challenges. The winning school will bring honor and prestige to their academy."

Orion's stomach churned at the thought of participating in such an important competition, his hands growing clammy. He repeated to himself, "Not me, not me, oh please don't choose me."

Elara shifted in her seat on the bench. "Can you believe it? The Otherworld Triad Tournament. I mean, I've heard stories, but being here to see it? That's next-level cool! Just think of the incredible magic we'll get to witness."

"Uh, yeah, that's one way to put it," Orion replied, giving a nervous chuckle. "I just hope we're not the ones tossed into that arena."

"Lighten up. This will make the chosen few legends." Ivy nudged him playfully with her elbow.

Orion didn't want to be a legend. He just wanted to survive high school at a magical academy and hone his plant magic abilities. His chest tightened, and he glanced around the room, silently praying that he wouldn't be selected.

Headmistress Nightshade tapped the podium with a wand, silencing the excited murmurs. "We understand this announcement has generated much anticipation and enthusiasm. However, please remember that our primary goal is to represent Charmcaster Academy with dignity and honor. Win or lose."

"Of course, Headmistress," chorused the students, their expressions a mix of solemnity and barely concealed excitement. It seemed fair to say that half were excited and the other half, like Orion, wanted to run and hide.

"Furthermore," the headmistress continued, her gaze sweeping over the crowd, "participating in the tournament is both a privilege and a responsibility. Those selected must train diligently, learn from our esteemed professors, and support their fellow competitors."

"Understood, Headmistress," the students replied in unison.

Orion's heart raced as he listened to the headmistress's words. The gravity of the situation weighed heavily on him. Should he be chosen, he would have to represent his school and uphold its honor—a daunting task for someone who still questioned the extent of his own abilities. *"You're tougher than you think."*

"Headmistress Nightshade is right," Elara whispered to Orion. "This is a tremendous responsibility, but it's also an incredible opportunity. Just imagine what we could learn!"

Orion nodded, trying to focus on the positive aspects of the tournament. He couldn't deny that the prospect of learning advanced magic was tempting, but the thought of competing against skilled opponents still loomed over him like a dark cloud.

"You okay, Orion?" Ivy said, squeezing Orion's hand. "You look greener than a green bean."

"Um, yeah. It's just a lot to take in," Orion replied, his voice barely audible above the excited chatter filling the space. How is this only day two on campus? He thought.

"Before we proceed," Headmistress Nightshade continued, her voice echoing through the Great Hall, "I shall explain the selection process for the tournament. As some of you may know, each of the three schools will send six first-year students to compete. We will choose these participants through a magical lottery."

"Magical lottery?" Elara whispered.

"Yeah," Flint said. "I heard about it from my older brother when he attended the academy."

"We inscribed each student's name on a small, enchanted piece of parchment. We have placed these within an antique vase." Headmistress Nightshade gestured to an ornate silver urn on the stage, its intricate carvings shimmering in the candlelight. "The vessel contains a powerful selection spell that ensures fairness and impartiality."

As the students murmured amongst themselves, Headmistress Nightshade raised a hand for silence. "We shall begin."

With bated breath, the assembled students watched as Headmistress Nightshade approached the urn. She reached into the vase, drawing out a single parchment, and then let it go. As it floated in the air and unrolled, it glowed with a soft, golden light, revealing a name written in elegant script.

"Orion Evergreen," Headmistress Nightshade announced, her voice carrying through the hall even without a microphone.

A mixture of shock and dread washed over Orion as he realized he had been chosen. His hands shook, and he could feel the weight of the gazes from his fellow students. Beside him, Ivy squeezed his arm, while Elara smiled at him.

Flint gave him a firm clap on the back. "You got this, dude," Flint whispered.

"Yeah, uh-huh," Orion replied, swallowing hard. How and why was he chosen? And why was he the first one chosen? This never would have happened had he stayed in the Evergreen's attic.

Once the initial surprise had subsided, Headmistress Nightshade reached into the urn again. This time, the parchment unfurled to reveal another name bathed in the same golden light.

"Elara Silverwind," she announced.

The students erupted in a cacophony of cheers and applause.

Elara looked stunned, yet overjoyed. Her eyes were wide as she glanced at Orion and smiled wide.

"Congratulations, Elara!" Ivy exclaimed, pulling her into a tight hug. "This is amazing!"

"Thank you," Elara replied. "I just hope I can kick some butt with my wind magic."

Ivy added, "And I'd love to see some awesome girl power battle it out."

Headmistress Nightshade selected two more names, Zara Pyre and Flint Rockwell.

The Great Hall buzzed with energy as students and faculty alike shared their thoughts on the upcoming Otherworld Triad Tournament. Excited chatter filled the air, punctuated by bursts of laughter and animated hand gestures.

Flint sat back. "We're on the same team, bro."

"Yeah, great," Orion mumbled.

Orion's worries increased tenfold. He shuddered at the idea of facing off against someone not only powerful with magic but able to control it. His abilities and capabilities felt minuscule compared to his classmates.

"Orion, relax," Ivy said sweetly. "You're an amazing plant Charmcaster and you'll do fine in the tournament."

Flint gave Orion a friendly smack on the back. "Come on, dude, a bit of rivalry is good for the soul."

Orion rolled his eyes, glancing sideways at Flint. "Sure, easy for you to say," he grumbled. Flint's knack for moving earth and stone seemed way more impressive than his humble plant magic. "You can literally move mountains whereas I can make a rose bloom." He knew he shouldn't compare himself to others. His mom scolded him often for this, but in this case, the difference between him and Flint was pretty huge.

As the noise in the Great Hall began to die down, Headmistress Nightshade stepped forward once more. "Let us all congratulate these special students on their selection," she paused, her voice stern yet warm. "And remember, they will represent not only Charmcaster Academy, but also each and every one of you. We must all support them in any way we can. United, we stand strong."

Orion's thoughts swirled like leaves caught in a whirlwind. His heart was pounding like a drumbeat, and his hands clammy with nerves. The weight of the upcoming Otherworld Triad Tournament bore down on him like an invisible force. Thoughts of failure and embarrassment filled his mind, threatening to consume him.

"I don't think I can do this," he murmured.

Ivy reached over, patting his shoulder. "Hey. You'll be awesome. You got this."

Flint crossed his arms. "Seriously, dude, once you start working your green magic out there, the competition won't even know what hit 'em."

Orion looked between them, their support easing his tension a bit. "Appreciate it, guys. I just... I don't wanna let down the headmistress or the school, you know?"

Ivy gave him a warm smile. "You won't, Orion. Trust in yourself, and we'll be there rooting for you all the way."

"*You're tougher than you think.*"

"Yeah," Elara said. "We're gonna be a team. We'll train together, we'll fight together. We've got this. We'll be the champs for the next four years, and they might even talk about us long after we graduate."

"Right," Orion said, taking a deep breath and

attempting to steady his nerves. No pressure. With his nerves all twisted up, all Orion wanted to do was run to his room.

Headmistress Nightshade tapped a wand-like stick against the podium again, commanding the attention of everyone. "Before we adjourn, I would like to summarize the magical training and duels that will take place during the preparation for the tournament," she said, her eyes scanning the crowd. "Professor Swiftwater has put together a rigorous training regimen that will push your magical abilities to new heights. We expect every student chosen for the Otherworld Triad Tournament to attend these after school lessons and give their utmost dedication to improving their skills."

Orion's nerves were just settling, but they flared anew as he considered the intensity of the training ahead. However, Ivy squeezed his hand reassuringly, and he felt a sense of peace wash over him. His hands felt hot and sweaty, but she didn't say anything.

"Lastly," the headmistress concluded, "this tournament is an opportunity to not only showcase your talents but also to learn from your peers. Embrace the experience, and may it serve to strengthen the bonds between our magical communities."

With that, Headmistress Nightshade nodded, signaling the end of her announcement.

Orion knew what was coming wouldn't be a cake-walk. But hey, with his gang backing him up and some of the top-notch teachers at Charmcaster Academy in his corner, he might be able to handle whatever wild stuff the Otherworld Triad Tournament would throw his way.

CHAPTER NINE

The Elysium Archive, the grand library at the center of Charmcaster Academy, had massive bookshelves that loomed over the library's visitors, housing a vast array of ancient tomes, spell books, and textbooks, each whispering the promise of untold knowledge. The air pulsed with magic, as shimmering dust motes danced around in the sunlight filtering through the high, stained-glass windows.

All around Elara, Orion, Ivy, and Flint were bookish spirits, specter-like librisprites that looked after the boundless collection. These otherworldly librarians moved in floating, fluid paths, effortlessly ascending the highest shelves to manage and catalog the magic-infused texts.

When Elara looked up from her textbook, she caught sight of bookworms, lizard-like creatures the size of rats, perched themselves on various shelves. Their scales glowed like the pages they protected, changing hues as they absorbed the contents of the books they rested upon. Their soft rustling and cooing noises added to the library's charm.

The group assembled at a round table in the back of the library, studying for an upcoming potion exam.

Orion sat hunched over a worn leather-bound book, his dark brown eyes narrowed behind his glasses as he read the faded script on the yellowed pages. "It says here that firedrake's scale is crucial for stabilizing volatile potions," he mumbled, his finger following the words on the page.

"Really?" Elara asked and leaned in closer to see the text, her white blonde hair cascading over her slender shoulders. "I thought it was used to amplify the effects."

"Another common misconception," Ivy said, her bright green hair bobbing as she nodded enthusiastically. "It can do both, but it depends on how you use it. You need to be very precise with your measurements. Precision is everything."

"Exactly," Flint agreed, his arms crossed defiantly. "One wrong move, and we'll have potions exploding in our faces. Not that it wouldn't be entertaining, but let's try to avoid the catastrophe, shall we? I kind of like my face."

Elara sighed, her brain fixed on the ancient tome, a focused energy radiating from her like waves of a powerful charm. She wanted to excel at Charmcaster Academy, and mastering the complexities of potion making was just a milestone on her magic-laden road to making a name for herself. She knew that passing this exam was important and it could knock the professors' socks off—literally if she wasn't careful.

"Let's go over the steps for the Elixir of Clarity again," Elara suggested, her eyes scanning the book intently. "We'll need to have this down perfectly for the exam."

Orion nodded, adjusting his glasses. "First, we heat the water to a rolling boil, then add the essence of moonflower and stir clockwise three times."

"Next, we sprinkle in the crushed belladonna berries and stir counterclockwise twice," Ivy said, her eyes closed as she recited the steps from memory.

"Then, we add the firedrake's scale, one pinch at a time, stirring continuously until the potion turns a deep blue," Flint added, flipping through the pages of his textbook.

Together, they continued their studies, their voices

mixed with the whispers of ancient magic and throughout the Elysium Archive, the rustle of turning pages was heard.

Elara had been engrossed in her reading when, out of nowhere, the book's text shifted and morphed. The once static letters danced around the pages, changing from words to elaborate diagrams that detailed complex magical processes. The book used an intricate illusion spell to illustrate the concepts it described.

"Look at the text," Orion murmured, nudging Elara gently. "I've never seen a book behave like this before."

"Strange," she agreed, smiling. "It's as if the book wants to help us pass the exam."

"Or maybe it's just reacting to our magical presence," Ivy suggested, her green eyes narrowing as she watched the text shimmer on the page.

"Or maybe it's a sign we should take a break," Flint added gruffly, rubbing his stiff neck. "We've been studying for hours."

"All right, let's call it a day," Ivy conceded, closing her book with a sigh, startling a nearby bookworm.

"Agreed," Flint said, gathering his books and notes and shoving them into his bag.

"See you tomorrow," Elara said.

Ivy and Flint waved goodbye as they headed off toward the dormitories.

Orion and Elara stayed seated and studied for a little longer. They were huddled in the back corner of the library when a deep, velvety voice broke through their whispering.

"My apologies for the interruption," said the beautiful woman standing over them. Her dark cloak of violet and black swirled around her like a tempest, shrouding her face in shadows and making the air dense, the fabric bleeding into the dim light of the library. "I am Professor Ember. I teach 'Advanced Magical Control' and I hope to see you in my course this year."

Professor Ember's gaze which seemed to bore into Orion. He felt suddenly powerless and could not move as she addressed him and Elara. "Hello, Professor," he managed, offering a small nod, his throat tight.

"Nice to meet you, ma'am," Elara said, her voice trembling slightly as she clutched her pencil tightly. Orion noted the fact that Elara's voice was a few octaves lower than usual.

"I noticed you two engrossed in your studies," she continued, her eyes flickering between them before settling on the open book on the table. Her lips twisted in a sly smirk that sent chills down Orion's spine. "Trying to impress the headmistress, perhaps?"

Elara cleared her throat. "Of course."

"That's an admirable goal," Ember replied. "Though knowledge isn't always found solely in books." She tapped the wooden table lightly with a slender finger, leaving behind an oppressive aura of shadows before fading back into the labyrinth of bookshelves.

The encounter left Orion feeling shaken and unsettled, making the pages of their book seem just a bit less significant than before. The librisprites peeked out around stacks of books, as if to make sure the coast was clear.

Elara let out a breath, making a slight whistling sound. "That was intense. Professor Ember is intimidating," she admitted, still gripping her pencil too tightly.

Orion nodded, his eyes wide. "Yeah, no kidding. Felt like I was a moth being stared down by a bat. Not exactly a warm welcome to her or her class."

"You're not getting cold feet about 'Advanced Magical Control', are you?" Elara teased, trying to lighten the mood.

"No... maybe, yes." He shrugged, the tension in the air fading a bit. "Let's just get back to our studies."

After another hour had passed, Orion's stomach grumbled. When did he eat last?

"Man, I'm hungry," Orion said, patting his stomach. "But dinner isn't for another hour, according to the clock."

Elara turned to the clock and pointed. "Which clock? Because they are all different. See?"

Orion tilted his head and pushed up his glasses. "Yeah, I see. Well, my stomach could care less which clock I look at as long as I put something in it pretty soon."

"We could grab a snack at one of the vending machines," Elara suggested.

He pushed back his chair. "Sounds like a plan." His hand dove into his pocket and he pulled out some folded dollar bills and some coins. "I think I have enough for both of us."

They walked along the corridor together, occasionally passing other students or teachers. The walls lined with antique tapestries depicting mythical creatures and powerful enchantments, their colors long faded but no less mesmerizing.

"How much further?" Orion asked. "I'm starving to death. I heard you get slices of pizza from the vending machines."

"I'm not sure," Elara admitted, her fingers trailing

over the tattered surface of the ancient wall hangings. "But I think it's around that corner past the artifact vault."

As they rounded a corner, she caught sight of the heavy wooden door leading to the vault—its surface adorned with intricate carvings of runes and sigils — sat slightly ajar.

"I wonder who left the door open," Elara said, pushing open the door wider with her hand. "Professor Mistral?"

The hinges creaked loudly, protesting the intrusion. Elara poked her head into the room when more of the space came into view. She saw it was bathed in an ethereal blue glow.

On the floor was the lifeless form of their beloved teacher, Professor Mistral. The air in the room was thick with a choking sense of dread and foreboding.

"Professor Mistral!" Elara gasped, her heart constricting painfully in her chest. She rushed into the room, followed by Orion.

"Is she okay?" Orion asked as he crouched to check her pulse. "Her skin is ice cold" He stood up abruptly and backed away. "Elara, we need to tell Headmistress Nightshade, like we need to get someone now!" he said urgently, his voice trembling with shock and fear.

In response to their call of distress, a magnificent owl materialized before them. Elara recognized the owl as a Moonseer. It was swathed in snowy white plumage and its eyes were like twin moons, deep and luminescent.

"Young Charmcasters, this is no place for you," the Moonseer warned.

Elara extended a shaky finger toward the lifeless body of Professor Mistral. "She's hurt, I think. What should we do? She needs help!"

The owl's gaze flickered to the professor's body. "An unfortunate occurrence. The headmistress should be notified immediately."

"Can you help us alert the headmistress?" Orion said, his voice wobbly. "I think... she might be dead."

The Moonseer bobbed its ivory head, its eyes flickering with the reflection of raw shock. "I shall find her right away," it intoned gravely. "Stay here."

And with a flash akin to a shooting star, the owl flew away, leaving Elara and Orion alone with the professor.

As they waited for help to arrive, Elara couldn't tear her eyes away from the lifeless form of Professor Mistral, her mind racing with questions and fears. The room seemed to pulse with an eerie silence. Elara couldn't even hear her own breathing or heartbeat, even though both were hammering with adrenaline.

How had this happened? Who could have done such a terrible thing? And most importantly, why?

Elara, her heart not slowing its staccato rhythm, watched Orion, his brow furrowed, examined the room with a disquieting intensity. They needed to know if a threat was here and whether or not they might be next.

His is attention dropped to the floor where a strange plant sat near the professor's body. A shiver raced down Elara's spine as she followed his gaze to the oddly dark, prickly flora.

"Orion," she breathed out, "What is that...?"

Orion's fingers hovered over the dark, prickly plant, careful not to touch. He looked up, his face as pale as Elara's hair. "This," he said, his voice barely above a whisper, "is a rare Nocturne Nettle."

Elara frowned as she tried to recall it. The name was vaguely familiar, a whispered detail in a long, exhaustive list of magical flora. "What's it doing in here?"

Orion's gaze remained locked on the plant. He swallowed hard, the action audible in the vault's silence. "I don't know," he said. "It's a potent ingredient used in some of the more advanced spells. And it for sure doesn't belong here in the artifact vault."

"Then why is it here?" Elara pointed out, her mind racing.

"Wish I knew," Orion said. "But that's not the most disturbing part."

"What?" Elara asked, the queasy feeling in the pit of her stomach only growing.

Orion finally tore his eyes away from the Nocturne Nettle, looking at her with a troubled expression. "This plant, Elara, is not native to Mythos Isle. It doesn't grow here naturally. Someone must've brought it into the vault with intent."

Elara took a step back, her heart pounding in her chest as she tried to decipher the uneasy sensation creeping over her. It was as if the air itself was holding its breath, stagnant and lifeless. She glanced toward Professor Mistral's shadow, stretching grotesquely across the cold marble floor, and the abnormal stillness around it struck her, so profound it was almost palpable.

The hairs on her neck prickled. As a wielder of wind magic, Elara was sensitive to the ebbs and flows of air currents. And this was not natural. Air was meant to move, to breathe, and yet here it was, frozen around the shadow as if time itself had stopped.

"Orion," she said, her voice catching on his name. Her hand moved in small circles as if trying to stir the stubborn air. "Something's not right. The air around her shadow...it's unnaturally still."

Orion, engrossed in his examination of the Nocturne Nettle, looked up. He frowned, an echo of her concern reflected in his eyes. "What do you mean?"

Elara looked back at the shadow, her mind wrestling with the puzzle. She bit her lower lip, a knot of unease forming in her stomach. "It's like they have sucked the air out of it," she said, "completely stagnant. I've only heard of this happening when casting the darkest spells."

Her voice trailed off, her eyes meeting Orion's in shared confusion and worry. The discovery of the Nocturne Nettle and now the static air over the shadow—their school wasn't feeling so safe anymore.

"The air, everything feels altered, doesn't it?" he said.

"Altered." Yes, that was the word she was looking for. "By dark magic," she said. The words tasted sour on her dry tongue.

Orion swallowed hard. "I think you might be right, Elara." He drew up a hand and pointed at her.

"What?" Elara asked, wondering what else could freak her out.

"Your hair. It's so straight."

Elara reached up and found her hair to be hanging straight down, perfectly smooth.

"Orion, this isn't good. Where is that bird? We need a professor." Tears of fear were on the edge of her voice as she pleaded.

Professor Mistral's life wasn't extinguished naturally. It seemed deliberate, calculated, and carried out with evil intent.

The weight of their discovery settled heavily upon them, leaving Elara and Orion feeling even more helpless and frightened. They couldn't ignore the fact that someone at Charmcaster Academy was dabbling in the dark arts.

As they stood there, lost in their thoughts and fears, Elara prayed that help would arrive soon. She couldn't bear the thought of being in that room any longer, with the lifeless body of their beloved professor and the ancient secrets surrounding them in here.

Finally, the sound of hurried footsteps echoed down the corridor, breaking the heavy silence that fell over Elara and Orion. Headmistress Nightshade appeared with three solemn-looking men in tow, their expressions grim as they took in the grisly scene within the artifact vault.

"Elara, Orion," the headmistress's voice was calm

but firm as she addressed them. "Please wait outside in the corridor while we examine the room."

As they exited the room, one of the three men closed the door behind them, effectively shutting out the sight of Professor Mistral.

Elara leaned against the cold stone wall of the hallway, the chill seeping through her robe, grounding her. Her breath hitched, the air coming out in short, frantic bursts. She pressed her hand against her chest, the pounding of her heart pulsating under her fingertips. It felt like a wild creature, frantic and desperate to escape its cage.

Never in her wildest nightmares had she imagined witnessing something like this. Death was something she'd read about in her spell books, a fact of life in the context of old Charmcasters who'd lived their full magical span. Never someone she knew. And why Professor Mistral, who just yesterday lectured them on the correct pronunciation of a complicated casting of a tornado spell.

Orion stood beside her, his eyes focused on the floor, his fingers nervously playing with the hem of his robe, lost in his own thoughts.

A lump formed in her throat, making it hard to swallow. A strange, heavy dread was sinking in her stomach, pulling her down. Her mind was a storm of thoughts, questions, fear, all of them crashing into each other, creating chaos she didn't know how to navigate. Out of resolve, Elara let herself sink to the floor.

The hallway was so quiet it felt like a vacuum, suffocating her like a thick blanket. It was a grave reminder of what had just happened, and that someone had died made Elara's skin crawl. She squeezed her eyes shut, but the image of Professor Mistral's lifeless body kept flashing through her mind in lurid color.

Elara pressed her head against the cold stone wall, trying to calm the frantic beating of her heart. She couldn't let this moment break her down, or worse yet, define her. From the ashes of fear and uncertainty, hope bloomed within her like a small flame, urging her to stay strong.

Unable to resist the urge to know more, Elara inched her butt closer to the door, pressing her ear against the wood. She could hear the murmur of voices inside, but only caught snippets of conversation.

"...a tragic accident," Headmistress Nightshade's voice was filled with sorrow. "We must notify her family immediately."

"Yes, ma'am," the man agreed solemnly. "For now, let us preserve the scene and ensure no further harm comes to our students."

She felt a hand on her shoulder. "Elara..." Orion warned, his voice barely audible. "We shouldn't be eavesdropping."

"Shush," Elara whispered and shrugged off his grip.

"One of the relics must have had an overflow of power and it was too much to withstand..." the headmistress replied.

"Most likely..." the man said.

Elara pulled away from the door. "Orion, they're talking about it being an accident. But we both know it wasn't."

"We don't know anything for certain," Orion said. "Let's wait until they finish their examination before jumping to conclusions. They know magic, let alone ancient magic, better than we do."

The door opened again, and Headmistress Nightshade emerged from the doorway, her face as hard and cold as the castle walls. Three stern-looking men followed, their steps echoing ominously in the corridor.

"Elara, Orion, are you alright? You weren't

harmed?" she asked, her tone gentle yet firm. The two of them shook their heads. She seemed to tower over them, her eyes reflecting a weighty understanding of the world they were yet to fully comprehend. "Good. This is a heavy burden for you both, but it's crucial that you return to your rooms. Allow us to handle the investigation. We'll get to the bottom of Professor Mistral's... *accident*. Till it becomes an official announcement, please be discreet with this...*information*."

"Headmistress," Elara said. "We don't believe it was an accident. In the vault, Orion and I saw—."

A swift hand shot up from the headmistress, cutting her off mid-sentence. "Elara," she warned, her voice dropping to a chilling whisper. Her gaze, usually so warm and inviting, was now a blockade, closed off and unyielding. "Do not speculate or start any rumors until we know more, please."

Orion fists balled at his sides. "The things we noticed... they just don't add up to an accident."

"Students," she said firmly. "Go back to your dorms now. I'm not discussing this with you." Headmistress Nightshade regarded them for a moment, her gaze flicking between Elara and Orion, before she pivoted to leave.

Elara wouldn't let her escape so easily. "Wait," she

blurted, a trace of desperation in her voice. "You're not even going to hear us out?"

Headmistress Nightshade paused, and for a heartbeat, Elara thought she had reached her. The headmistress turned back around, her gaze meeting Elara's determined stare. "I have heard you, Elara. But we have specialists for these matters," she replied with an air of finality.

"But they won't find what we did," Orion said, taking a step forward, his expression hardening. "There was a Nocturne Nettle inside the vault. It's a plant that doesn't even grow on Mythos Isle."

For the first time, a flicker of surprise crossed Headmistress Nightshade's face, but it was quickly replaced by her typical stoic expression. "I understand your concern, Orion. However, our botanical experts are highly trained. If what you're saying is true, we'll look into it."

"And what about the stillness in the air?" Elara shot back, folding her arms in a defensive stance. "I felt it around Professor Mistral's shadow. That's not normal, Headmistress. It felt like the result of a dark spell."

Now, it was the headmistress's turn to fold her arms in defiance. She gave Elara a long look before finally saying, "You aren't trained yet on how to identify the nuances of spells, Elara. What you felt may well have resulted from your distress."

"But what if we're right?" Orion demanded. His voice echoed down the corridor, a plea absorbed by the castle. "What if it's more than an accident?"

There was a moment of silence. Finally, Headmistress Nightshade sighed, a tired, world-weary sound. "Let's hope, for all our sakes, that you're wrong. Now, please, go to your rooms."

And with that, she turned and disappeared down the corridor, leaving Orion and Elara standing alone amidst a sea of unanswered questions.

Elara clenched her fists at her sides. She could feel the familiar sensation of wind magic tingling in her fingertips, her emotions threatening to unleash a whirlwind. But now wasn't the time for that. Instead, she forced herself to take a deep, calming breath, her intuition telling her that something just wasn't right.

"Orion," she whispered, turning to her friend. "Do you really believe that Professor Mistral's death was just an accident?"

The boy shook his head slowly, his eyes downcast behind his black-framed glasses. "No," he admitted quietly. "It doesn't add up. It was no accident."

"Exactly," Elara said, her voice barely audible.

As they walked through the dimly lit corridors

toward their dormitories, Elara's heart felt heavy with frustration and sorrow. She couldn't shake the feeling that something much more sinister lay hidden beneath the surface of Professor Mistral's so-called accident.

And she knew, without a doubt, that she wouldn't rest until she uncovered the truth.

CHAPTER TEN

Orion noticed how time passed weirdly at Charmcaster Academy. They filled his days with magic and lessons, each one bleeding into the next. It was hard to keep track of the weeks, but every time he passed by that withering ivy in herbology class, it reminded him of how things had changed since Professor Mistral had passed away. The ivy used to be vibrant, full of life, just like the school. Now, it was more like a visual echo of the dark cloud that had settled over everyone. Sleep wasn't any better. Nights were full of restless tosses and turns, and there were dreams where he was running through an endless forest, the face of the murdered professor following him in the shadows.

The more he tried to focus on learning magic, the

more this murder mystery crept into his thoughts, tarnishing the thrill he once had of being in the academy. It was like an annoying buzz in his ear that wouldn't stop, reminding him that all wasn't well in their magical world.

Icy dread seeped into his bones, as if the vault's chill had latched onto him, refusing to let go. A wave of nausea rose in him, swirling the pit of his stomach. He gulped, swallowing down the unsettling feeling, the taste of his half-eaten lunch turning sour in his mouth. For a moment, he closed his eyes, hoping to eclipse the scene that haunted him, but the darkness behind his eyelids only made the image more vivid.

Blowing out a breath, he opened his eyes and kept walking toward the courtyard to meet his friends.

Orion turned a corner in the dimly lit hallway, coming to an abrupt halt when he spotted two figures ahead. The faint glow of the enchanted wall sconces revealed Professor Ember, her dark cloak swirling around her like a tangible shadow. Beside her stood a colleague, their back to Orion.

Orion thought that Professor Ember was stunningly beautiful and the coolest, scariest woman he'd ever met. She had flawless dark olive skin, hypnotic brown eyes, killer cheekbones, and glossy black hair streaked with cool lavender highlights. Ember had a lithe figure and was of average height, but she had this way of holding herself that just demanded attention. She wore flowing black and violet robes that seemed to merge with the surrounding shadows, and Orion felt a mix of admiration and trepidation watching her.

Ember's hand flexed open and closed around an object that gleamed even in the scarce light. It looked to be the shape of a key. Its surface was inscribed with intricate designs and symbols that Orion couldn't quite make out. He strained to listen to their conversation, tucking himself behind a stone pillar.

"I trust you understand the implications of this." The swirl of shadows around Ember seemed to intensify with every syllable, like an ominous dance of darkness.

"Naturally," the other teacher replied, their voice shaking slightly.

Orion watched as the shadows seemed to writhe and curl around Ember, almost as if they were a part of her. The sight was terrifying, yet fascinating, her suspicious demeanor as elusive as the night itself.

When Ember and the other teacher turned to leave, Orion pressed his back against the pillar and held his breath, staying hidden until their footsteps faded away.

Then he rushed out of the castle and onto a path surrounding the courtyard.

Today, the quad was bustling with students, their somber expressions and hushed conversations filling the crisp fall air. The sun cast a golden glow on the ancient structures around them, each adorned with twisting ivy. Gargoyles perched upon the high parapets, their solid forms subtly shifting and stretching their rocky limbs amidst the stonework.

The courtyard bloomed with an explosion of vibrant flowerbeds, bursting with colors and shapes in intricate geometric patterns. Amidst the foliage, students gathered at the grand fountain, their feet becoming the unsuspecting targets of mischievous water sprites. Laughter echoed through the air as the sprites tickled their toes, leaving them both amused and dry.

Orion stood near one of four arched entrances, his body hidden behind a thick marble column. He clutched a worn backpack tightly against his chest, as if it could shield him from the world. His brown eyes darted about nervously from one group of students to another.

"Hey, Orion!" Ivy called out from across the courtyard.

Orion's head snapped up, searching for the source of the greeting.

"Over here, plant dude!" Flint yelled, standing up.

Orion spotted Flint, waving enthusiastically among a group of their friends, Elara, Ivy, Aria, Cyrus, and Zara, all sitting on the grass near a towering oak tree. With a deep breath, Orion forced himself to take a step forward, then another, until he was walking hesitantly toward them. He reminded himself to smile and not act weird.

"Hi, guys," he muttered, his gaze fixed firmly on the ground as he approached.

"Hey, you made it!" Flint said, clapping him on the back with enough force to make Orion stumble slightly. "We were thinking you'd never leave your room."

"Sorry," Orion mumbled, his cheeks burning with embarrassment. "I was studying and must've lost track of time. I should have come out here sooner. This weather is perfect."

"Lost in your plants, you mean?" Ivy teased, her bright green hair ruffling against her collar as she teased.

Orion smiled at her. "Um, yeah," he admitted, rubbing the back of his neck self-consciously. "You know how it is."

They were all quiet a moment as Orion sat down and Flint took a seat closer to the tree.

"I keep thinking about Professor Mistrial," Aria said softly. "That must've been awful."

Orion's expression darkened, still haunted by the image of Professor Mistral's lifeless body sprawled on the cold stone floor of the vault. Even now, surrounded by his friends, he couldn't shake the tremors that gripped him. He swallowed hard, trying to push the memory aside and focus on the present.

"Orion, you okay?" Elara asked, her stare filled with concern as she studied his face, her hair pulled back into a tight ponytail.

"Y-yeah," Orion stammered, forcing a weak smile. "Just tired and still a little weirded out."

Orion looked over at Cyrus sprawled out on the grass, his light-brown hair catching the sun's rays. With a thick paperback clutched firmly in his hands, he remained engrossed, as if oblivious to the world around him.

"About finding the body?" Flint asked, his stout, muscular frame tense as he leaned against the tree. His square face was set in a grim expression, betraying his own unease beneath his tough exterior. "Dude, that was like weeks ago."

"Yeah," Orion said. "That's not something you

forget overnight." His hoarse words echoed the unease they all felt. "Finding Professor Mistral like that. It just doesn't make sense."

"Who wouldn't be freaked out?" Aria said, her tall, slender figure sitting elegantly in a yoga pose. Her heart-shaped face framed by long, wavy blonde hair, her pale skin almost luminescent in the sunshine.

"Guys, we shouldn't dwell on it," Ivy interjected. She squeezed Orion's hand gently, her eyes full of empathy. "It's sad, but these things happen."

"Precisely," Cyrus agreed, lowering his book a fraction to peer over the binding. "It's not like any of us can do anything about it, anyway." He lifted the book again and continued to read.

"Maybe not," Zara said, her curvy, medium-built frame leaning against the trunk of the oak. Her pretty face was outlined by straight black hair with vibrant red highlights, her rich brown skin glowing. "But it doesn't mean we can't feel for our fallen professor."

"They're saying it was an accident," Elara said, her voice soft but firm, "but I don't believe that."

Orion's heart felt heavy. "Neither do I," he said soberly.

"Orion," Ivy said, then glanced at the others before lowering her voice. "What do you think happened to

Professor Mistral? I mean, how did an artifact kill her?"

"I don't know," Orion admitted, his fingers twitching as he remembered the cold touch of her skin beneath his trembling fingers. He wished he could forget it all, but something etched the images into his mind like scars that refused to fade. "But when Elara and I were taking a tour of the vault with Professor Mistrial, a relic released a dangerous burst of magic, so that might be what happened."

Aria sighed, "To think I was jealous that you got to go in there. Cuz now? I am never going in there. Ever." She flicked a stray strand away from her pale face with an air of impatience. "Do we really need to talk about this now? It's so morbid."

"It sucks," Flint grumbled, crossing his muscular arms over his chest. His square face remained unyielding, betraying no sympathy for Orion's feelings. "But our focus should be on learning magic, not getting tangled up in mysteries. Let the authorities deal with it."

"I guess Flint has a point," Ivy said, her fingers twirling through her vibrant green bobbed hair. She shifted uncomfortably, her expression showing her unease. "We'll miss Professor Mistrial, but we can't dwell on it. We have to keep pushing forward."

"And we could get into trouble for poking our nose where it doesn't belong," Cyrus said, lowering his book. "Hopefully, the headmistress will keep this from happening again."

"Enough," Zara said in a shaky voice. "It's terrible, but we're not detectives, we're students. Can we please change the subject?"

The others seemed to agree, but Orion could see the flicker of curiosity still dancing in Elara's eyes. He knew she was the type—like him—that wouldn't let this go until she had answers.

"Fine," Elara conceded. "I promise not to bring it up again."

"Attention, students!" Headmistress Nightshade's voice boomed over the loudspeaker attached to a stone column holding a lantern. It startled everyone into silence. "It is with grave concern I inform you that an ancient relic, Aegis of the Ancients, has been reported missing from the artifact vault."

A collective gasp echoed throughout the courtyard. Orion sat up and pushed up his glasses. He flashed a shocked look in Elara's direction.

"Guards will be stationed at all entrances and exits of the vault immediately," the headmistress continued, her voice stern. "I advised students to remain vigilant and report any suspicious activity to the nearest faculty member. As an extra precaution, use the buddy system when out of your dorm room."

As the announcement concluded, the courtyard erupted into concerned whispers and speculation about the missing artifact.

Hoping no one noticed, Elara scooted her butt and books closer to Orion. "Missing?" Elara whispered, her brows furrowed in concern. "How could that be?"

Orion shrugged, his mind racing to comprehend the situation. He worried that the theft of Aegis of the Ancients and Professor Mistral's death were somehow connected. And the thought made his stomach twist uncomfortably.

"You don't think it's got anything to do with... Professor Mistral, do you?" Orion's voice was hushed as he pondered a chilling possibility.

"I'm kinda leaning that way, yeah," Elara admitted, biting her lower lip.

"Come on, it might just be a freaky coincidence," Flint said, though he didn't look too sure himself.

"But who would swipe it?" Zara threw her hands up in exasperation. "And why?"

"Coincidence or not, something's totally off here," Elara said.

Orion nodded, swallowing hard. "But how does

anyone snatch something like a powerful artifact, and nobody sees it happen?"

"And what about us?" Ivy added, her eyes looking almost as green as her name. "A professor drops dead out of nowhere, and now the relic's AWOL? Are we even safe in this place? My mom will freak out when she learns about this."

Cyrus, who had been quiet throughout most of the conversation, looked up from his book. "Of course, we're safe," he said, though he couldn't quite hide the concern that flickered in his stormy gaze. "The faculty will sort this out, and everything will be back to normal soon enough."

"Let's hope you're right," Orion said, his fingers clenched around the worn fabric of his backpack strap. His mind churned with thoughts about Professor Mistral's untimely death. The image of her dead body etched into his mind's eye was as clear as if he was still standing in the chilling vault.

He clenched his jaw, his knuckles paling around his backpack strap. He needed to keep it together. For himself. For Elara. For everyone at Charmcaster Academy. But the challenge felt as daunting as climbing the highest peak of Mythos Isle without a map or compass.

His friends stood up, except Elara. They mumbled goodbyes and said they had homework to finish. Once they had vanished back inside the castle, Orion sighed with relief.

Elara's gaze swept across the courtyard, the warm afternoon sun casting a golden glow on her angelic face. "Orion, we can't ignore this," she said, her voice filled with intensity. "We should conduct our own investigation."

Orion's eyes flickered with uncertainty as he surveyed the ancient stone buildings that surrounded them. "But Elara, we're just students," he muttered, his voice tinged with hesitation. "Shouldn't we trust the faculty to handle it?"

Elara's voice cut through the air, resolute and unyielding. "Think about it, Orion," she urged. "The thief stole Aegis of the Ancients right under their noses. We can't afford to sit back while the culprit remains at large."

The gravity of her words made his pulse pound in his ears. Was it possible that someone within the academy had committed such a heinous act?

"What if they're not able to solve this on their own? We could help," Elara insisted, placing a hand on his shoulder. "Don't you want to find out what really happened?"

Orion hesitated, torn between his desire to uncover the truth and his fear of getting caught up in something much larger than himself. "*You're tougher than you think.*" His stomach churned with anxiety, but there was no denying the spark of curiosity that just ignited within him.

"All right," he finally agreed, his voice barely audible. "But we need to be careful. If anyone finds out we're snooping around, we could get into serious trouble."

"Agreed." Elara nodded as she refrained from reaching out and squeezing Orion into a big hug.

The courtyard was emptying as their fellow students headed off to late afternoon classes or study hall, leaving Orion and Elara sitting alone amidst the swirling leaves and crisp fall air.

Without even giving it much thought, Elara waved a finger in the air. Two leaves blew up from the grass around her and she made them dance by using a small twirl of the fall air.

"Oh! I have an idea." Elara withdrew her hand, letting the leaves fall. Dropping her voice to a conspiratorial whisper, she said, "We can start researching the plant and the shadowy stillness we found in the vault. They have to be in a book somewhere."

Orion's breath fogged up his glasses as he hesitated, his heart pounding in his chest. "Okay, gotcha. The library might help us figure out what spell they may have used."

"Yes! Good idea." His new best friend reached out, gently placing a hand on his arm. "I know you're scared, Orion, but we can't just stand by and let this go unsolved."

"I know," he muttered, wiping his glasses on the hem of his jacket. "But what if we get caught? What if we make things worse?"

Elara smiled softly, squeezing his arm reassuringly. "We'll be careful. Besides, we have each other, and our magic, to help us. If we stick together, we can uncover the truth. Doesn't Professor Mistral deserve that much?"

Orion stared at the ground for a moment, considering her words. Professor Mistral deserved justice, and perhaps they were the only ones who could provide it.

Swallowing hard, Orion nodded, his resolve growing stronger. "Okay, I'm in. Let's do this."

"Really?" Elara's eyes lit up. "You mean it?"

"Of course," Orion replied, attempting to sound more confident than he felt.

Elara grinned, her face shining with admiration and gratitude. "We'll solve this mystery together."

Feeling a newfound sense of purpose, Orion met Elara's enthusiastic gaze with a smile. He felt like an equal partner in something important, not merely a sidekick or a tag-along. The truth behind Professor Mistral's death and the vanished Aegis of the Ancients was within their reach.

They stood and dusted themselves off. Stepping into the school, Orion's mind buzzed with questions. Who was responsible for the murder? What was the motive? How did it tie to the missing artifact? And, perhaps most dauntingly, were they ready to face the consequences of uncovering such dangerous secrets?

Regardless, they would find the answers and bring justice to their fallen professor.

CHAPTER ELEVEN

As Elara stepped into the grand, high-domed room that served as their Advanced Magical Control classroom, she felt a sense of awe. The semi-circle of desks seemed to curl protectively around the students, as if welcoming them into its embrace. Sunlight filtered through the stained-glass windows that lined the walls, bathing the room in a spectrum of colors.

She scanned the room, spotting her classmates, Zara, Ivy, Aria, and Cyrus, who were already gathered in a corner and chatting amongst themselves. Someone adorned the walls with ancient symbols and intricate designs that seemed to be woven with magic. The sweet scent of incense filled the room, along with magical herbs and the faint aroma of leather-bound books.

"Hey, Elara!" Aria called out with a bubbly tone as she waved. "How are you feeling about today's lesson?"

"Excited, but a little nervous too," Elara admitted. She moved closer to a desk and set her backpack on the seat. "I'm hoping to enhance my wind magic."

"I can't wait to see you in action," Ivy said, her bright green hair and eyes making her look like she had just stepped out of a lush forest. "Your affinity for wind is so cool."

"Speaking of unique affinities," Cyrus said, leaning against his desk with an air of nonchalance. His stormy gray eyes flickered to each of them. "Rumor has it our new professor, the mysterious Professor Ember, has some pretty fascinating abilities herself."

"It's true. Only six months, and Ember's already become something of a legend around here," Zara remarked, the fiery red streaks in her straight black hair matching her haughty attitude. "Heard she can control shadows like no one else."

"Umbrakinesis, they call it," Aria added, her voice barely above a whisper. She ran a finger along the spines of the books on the table. "Super rare stuff. A powerful form of darker magic."

"Huh." Elara leaned back against her chair, crossing her arms. "What else do you know?"

Ivy gave an awkward shrug, worrying her bottom lip between her teeth. "Well, she's not exactly social, and super strict. There's just... I dunno, something is weird about this Professor Ember."

"What do you mean?" Elara pressed, her interest truly hooked now.

Cyrus cleared his throat, leaning in closer to the group. In a low, conspiratorial whisper he said, "Well, rumor has it that she can summon shadows at will... and use them to, you know, spy on students. Creepy, right?"

As the others nodded in agreement, Elara couldn't shake the uneasy feeling that instantly settled in her chest.

Elara noticed a plain book on her desk. Its worn cover bore no title, only the subtle trace of a faint, weathered emblem. With a mix of curiosity and caution, she gently lifted the cover. As the aged pages fell open, a surge of animated chatter burst from within. The text on the pages shifted as if looking up at Elara.

"Good day to you, Miss Elara!" a bold, flourishing script greeted from the top margin, letters stretching and bending with each spoken word.

"And how might we be assisting your studies today?" a more formal text inquired from a footnote.

A boisterous conversation, located in the middle of the page, caught her eye: a pair of quotation marks were embroiled in a heated debate with a semicolon over who was more critical to the narrative.

"Without us, they'd do not know who's speaking!" one quotation mark asserted with a cheeky twist of its curve.

"Nonsense!" the semicolon retorted, its top dot bobbing vehemently. "I provide the essential pause in thoughts. Therefore, I am indispensable!"

Laughter bubbled up from Elara as the written words continued their lively interactions, turning an otherwise plain book into an animated chatterbox of textual dialogues. It was a unique, magical slice of life at Charmcaster Academy that never ceased to amaze her, and she shut the book with a smile.

Elara summoned her magic and created a wind orb. She clenched her fists around the wind orb, its translucent surface shimmering sphere with an ethereal glow. It was an embodiment of the magic she longed to control—a swirling, restless energy that matched her own ambition. She released a slow breath, trying to center herself in the tense atmosphere.

"Nervous?" Ivy asked, glancing at Elara's hands.

"Not really," Elara said, the weight of her wind orb grounding her. "If I can learn to develop my magic, who knows what I'll be able to achieve?"

"That's how I feel," Aria said, her fingers tracing delicate patterns in the air as if the light wove itself into a glittering tapestry before her.

"Hey, look at that!" Cyrus exclaimed, pointing toward a corner of the room where a bookshelf came to life. Leather-bound tomes soared through the air, their pages flapping like wings as they darted and swooped in an intricate dance.

"That's baffling," Zara said, ducking as a book flew past her head. "Those books need to chill."

"Yeah, they do," Ivy said, taking a seat at a desk near Elara.

Elara felt a sense of friendship and brotherhood with the bond they all shared. They were all different —in appearance, in personality, and in the magic they wielded—but their commitment united them to mastering their powers and learning from each other.

She tightened her grip on the wind orb. She felt the familiar pulse of energy beneath her fingertips, as if the orb were a living, breathing thing.

The sudden squeaking of the classroom door diverted their attention. The door swung open to reveal Professor Ember. A tall, imposing figure with a stern expression interrupted the moment. Her entrance seemed to suck the warmth out of the room, leaving behind an icy chill that sent shivers down Elara's spine.

"Good morning, students," Professor Ember said, her voice cold and sharp. "It is time to take your magic a step further in my Advanced Magical Control class."

As she spoke, Elara admired the silk dress that the professor wore under her robe, draped in layers of dark hues that seemed to shift and liquify like the shadows themselves.

"Your previous training has no doubt taught you how to harness your powers," Professor Ember swept her gaze across the faces of her students. "But true mastery requires control, discipline, and a grasp of the consequences that come with wielding such power."

"Is she always this intense?" Aria murmured to Elara from the corner of her mouth.

Elara struggled to quell the unease that had taken root in her belly. No matter how hard she tried, something about the woman's presence unnerved her.

The professor paced slowly, her black robes flowing around her in an eerie spectacle of power. "Magic can be a double-edged sword," she said with conviction, her words like tendrils of fog curling around them. "In the right hands, it can bring about great wonders and accomplishments. But in the wrong hands, or when wielded without proper control, it can lead to disaster."

Elara glanced at the wind orb resting in her hand, the manifestation of her innate power. She felt its energy pulsing beneath her fingertips, a constant reminder of the incredible potential that lay within her —if only she could learn to harness it better.

"Throughout this course, we will explore techniques and methods for enhancing your magical abilities," Professor Ember explained, strolling around around the room as she spoke. "We will delve into the intricacies of hand gestures, incantations, and the mental focus required to wield your elemental gifts with precision and finesse."

"Sounds like a challenge," Cyrus whispered to Zara, a smirk on his face.

"Indeed, Mr. Stormbringer," Professor Ember said, having overheard his comment. "And challenges are what help us grow and realize our true potential. Do not take this course lightly, any of you. I expect nothing less than your full dedication and commitment."

As she finished speaking, Elara felt the weight of Professor Ember's penetrating gaze upon her, as if the woman could read her doubts like an open book. But instead of cowering under the scrutiny, Elara channeled it as a source of strength. She had a gale raging inside her that refused to be extinguished. She was going to master her wind magic, no matter what it took.

"Observe," Professor Ember commanded, her voice resonating in the vast chamber. With a graceful sweep of her arm, she gestured toward the floor, where shadows began to twist and dance beneath her feet. The slithering tendrils of darkness coiled around her legs like serpents, moving in tandem with her every step.

Elara's eyes widened at the display of magic, an anxiousness creeping into her heart.

"Umbrakinesis is a rare and powerful skill," Professor Ember said, and the shadows retreated to their original positions, as if they had never moved at all. "Not everyone possesses the ability to manipulate the darkness, but those who do must learn to control it, lest it consume them." She paused, her eyes locking onto Elara for a split second. "We shall begin today's lesson."

Elara's spine tingled as the professor's commanding voice cut through the air, sending a shiver down her spine.

"Did you see that?" Ivy whispered, her vibrant

green eyes wide with shock. "Those shadows were alive!"

"Alive or not, I wouldn't want to mess with her," Cyrus replied, his face pale beneath his usual bravado.

Professor Ember's voice sliced through the whispers, her tone brooking no further chatter. "Today, we shall delve into the foundations of magical control, starting with the simplest of exercises. Like Elara has done, create a sphere of magic in your hand that represents your elemental power."

As the lesson began, Elara felt the weight of her wind orb in her hands, its presence a constant reminder of her goals.

"Begin by extending your dominant hand," Professor Ember instructed, and Elara and her classmates mimicked her movement, each holding their spheres of power above their desks. "Now, close your eyes and focus on your personal connection to the elemental force within you."

Elara closed her eyes, concentrating on the orb in her hand. She could feel the energy thrumming within it, a reflection of her own affinity for wind magic. The air around her seemed to stir, as if summoned by her thoughts. A strand of hair blowing across her neck.

Professor Ember paced between the desks, her flowing robes floating just above the floor. As the students watched, she approached the chalkboard and began writing an incantation with swift, deliberate strokes. The ancient symbols glowed faintly as they appeared on the board, each stroke filled with a mystic energy that resonated in the air.

Professor Ember turned to face the class, her piercing gaze sweeping across the room. "Now, I want each of you to recite the incantation I've written. Remember, focus on the words and your deep connection to your element. Let the magic flow through you, intertwining your will with the very essence of your power."

As the students recited the incantation, Elara's senses sharpened. She could feel the air in the room shifting, growing more charged with every repetition. The gentle breeze that had once flowed harmoniously through the classroom now seemed restless, eager to break free from its confines. Elara tightened her grip on her orb, her brows furrowing in concentration as she struggled to maintain control over the increasingly unruly winds.

"Control your powers, Elara!" Professor Ember's stern voice broke through Elara's concentration. "Do not allow your magic element to control you, young lady."

Elara bit her lip, her face flushed with frustration.

She tried again, willing herself to regain control over the capricious winds, but the orb in her hand continued to shudder and jerk, its movements growing increasingly erratic.

"Look at Elara," Aria said, her eyes narrowed in worry. "She's really struggling."

"Shh," Ivy said harshly. "Don't distract her."

"Enough!" Professor Ember barked, her voice sharp and commanding.

The room fell silent as she moved toward Elara, her gaze fixed on the trembling wind orb in her hands.

"Elara, you must learn to master your emotions as well as your magic. The wind is a fickle element, easily swayed by the slightest shift in your focus."

Elara nodded, her heart pounding in her chest. She could feel the eyes of her classmates on her, their whispers fueling her persistence to regain control.

"Once more, Elara," Professor Ember instructed. "This time, envision harnessing the winds with your mind and guiding them through the orb."

Taking a deep breath, Elara closed her eyes and focused on the professor's words. She imagined the winds as an extension of herself, bending to her will as she channeled them through the orb. Slowly, she felt the erratic movements steady, the winds calming under her guidance.

Elara sighed. She had done it.

"Very good," Professor Ember said with a curt nod. "Magical control demands not only power but discipline and concentration. Now, let us continue our practice."

Elara's hands trembled and her heart pounded, the orb suddenly grew bigger and bigger.

In a burst of unexpected chaos, Elara's wind orb detonated in her palm, unleashing a tempestuous gust that whipped through the classroom. Ivy's emerald tresses became a wild, swirling canopy around her face, while Zara's fiery gaze widened in astonishment. Aria clung desperately to the moonlight she had been manipulating, using it as a shield against the miniature cyclone that threatened to engulf them all. Meanwhile, Cyrus scowled fiercely, his teeth clenched in defiance as he grappled with the tempestuous power of his own storm abilities.

"Everyone, stay calm!" Professor Ember called out. Her voice as sharp as a knife's edge. Her stern expression remained unchanged, even as shadows slithered beneath her feet, reacting to the tumultuous atmosphere. "Elara! You must regain control of your magic this instance!"

In the wake of the unleashed winds, the classroom transformed into a frenzy of fluttering papers, cascading books, and rattling desks. The once orderly stack of textbooks in the bookcase swayed precariously, threatening to topple like dominos. The curtains billowed and swirled like restless specters, their fabric dancing in sync with the howling gales that filled the room.

Elara's palms grew sweaty and her breath shallow. She felt the weight of her classmates' gazes upon her, only adding to the pressure. It was as if the very air itself had turned against her, mocking her inability to subdue it.

"Listen to my voice, Elara," Professor Ember said firmly. "Focus on the center of the whirlwind, where the winds are calmest. Draw upon that stillness and take back control."

Closing her eyes, Elara took a deep breath, focusing on the core of the whirlwind as instructed. Inhaling deeply, she felt the familiar tingle of her magical connection to the wind, like fine threads woven between her fingers and the churning air.

"Good," Professor Ember encouraged her. "Now, speak the incantation we practiced earlier again. Let the words guide your magic, allowing you to direct the winds as you see fit."

Elara whispered the spell, her voice barely audible

above the howling gale. The winds seemed to respond, their chaotic dance slowing ever so slightly.

"Again," Professor Ember urged, a hint of urgency entering her voice. "Louder this time. Assert your will over the winds, Elara. Remember, you are their master."

Elara spoke louder, her voice stronger and more confident. The whirlwind shrank, the winds gradually bending to her command. With one final shout, Elara forced the remaining gusts of air back into the now steady wind orb hovering above her palm.

"You need much more discipline, Elara," Professor Ember commended, her voice betraying no emotion. She turned to address the entire class. "I trust this has been a valuable lesson for all of you. Magical control requires not only raw power but also unwavering focus and discipline."

Elara felt a heavy disappointment in herself as her heart rate slowed, and her nerves settled.

Professor Ember's icy voice resonated across the classroom. "The homework for this week is chapters five and six. No excuses for late submissions." With a wave of her hand, the assignments floated out from a pile on her desk, swooping toward each student like scholarly birds, finally resting neatly in front of them.

"Dismissed," she said, a harsh finality in her tone while turning her back to her students.

The noise of rustling bags and hushed voices filled the room, chairs scraped against the floor, and students filed out of the classroom. Only then did Professor Ember's icy gaze fall on Elara, pinning her to the spot. "Miss Silverwind," she called. "A word before you leave, please."

Elara approached the imposing figure of Professor Ember. "Yes, Professor?"

"Your pathetic control over the winds is laughable," she sneered, her voice dripping with disdain. "It's clear you have no idea how to harness your element properly. If you continue like this, you'll only bring chaos and destruction."

Her words cut deep, a reminder of the responsibility that weighed heavily on her shoulders.

Elara nodded, swallowing hard. "Yes, Professor. I understand."

"See that you do." Professor Ember dismissed her with a wave of her hand. "You may go."

Exiting the classroom, Elara slipped into the bustling flow of students in the corridor, her friends immediately surrounding her.

"You okay, Elara?" Aria's question sliced through the hallway chatter.

Elara managed a small nod, tucking a stray lock of hair behind her ear. "Feeling overwhelmed. Need to work on my control, I guess." She willed herself not to cry. At least not till she was alone. She felt like they singled her out and that didn't sit well with her.

Cyrus, his easy-going grin never faltering, said, "Hey, we've all been there. Power hiccups are like magical puberty."

His joke coaxed a chuckle from Elara, her tense posture relaxing. "That's one way to put it."

Ivy rolled her eyes, but her voice was kind. "You'll nail it soon, Elara. You've got the talent. Don't let her scare you."

Zara, ever the quiet one, offered a supportive pat on Elara's shoulder. "We've got your back, Elara."

"Thanks, guys," Elara said, touched by their support.

As the corridor emptied, Elara cast one last glance back toward the ominous door of the classroom. She felt a jolt of resolve, her spirit unyielding despite the day's trials. She decided then and there; she wouldn't let a single setback hinder her journey at the Charmcaster Academy. After all, tomorrow was a new day. And she was ready for whatever magic it would bring.

CHAPTER TWELVE

The heavy oak door to Charmcaster Academy's Elysium Archive creaked open, revealing a cavernous library filled with towering bookshelves, ancient scrolls, and the musty scent of old parchment. The afternoon sun filtered through the vault's high stained glass windows, casting a kaleidoscope of colors onto the polished marble floors. Elara smiled at the sight of the librisprites.

"We need to discover why that rare flora, Nocturne Nettle, was in the artifact vault near the professor's body," Orion whispered, adjusting his black-framed glasses as he hesitated at the entrance. His brown eyes flickered between the imposing bookshelves and the resolute expression on his friend's face. "This is the best place to do research into unique plants and spells."

"And," Elara replied, her blue eyes gleaming with resolve, "we need to find out what that unnatural stillness in the air around the professor's shadow meant."

As they stepped into the hallowed halls of knowledge, Elara's blonde hair swirled around her like an ethereal halo, defying gravity in response to her emotions. She was keenly aware of the weight of the task before them, but her innate curiosity and determination to unravel the mysteries had steeled her resolve.

"Let's start in the magic flora section," Orion said beside her. "We might find more info on the Nocturne Nettle and its uses."

"Good idea," Elara said, her voice firm and reassuring.

Together, they ventured deeper into the labyrinthine archive, their footsteps echoing softly against the cool flooring. Orion's fingers traced the spines of dusty books, the air around them heavy with the scent of ancient parchment and ink.

"You study that rare plant text, and I'll do some research with these two books on magic plants and ancient floras." Orion said, scanning the countless volumes that lined the shelves.

"Okay," Elara said.

As the pair delved into their research, their whispers and rustling of pages melded with the ambient chorus of the library. Time seemed to stand still within the Elysium Archive, as if the knowledge housed within its walls held dominion over the passage of time.

In a quiet corner of the library, Elara looked up and saw Professor Ember, her eyes scanning the rows of ancient tomes with an intensity that made the air around her hum. The shadowy alcove she occupied seemed to darken, as if the very light around her was being absorbed by her dark robes. She traced a slender finger over the spine of an old, leather-bound book, her gaze intense as though she could decipher its secrets without cracking it open. Yet, as soon as a group of students entered the library, she straightened and sauntered away, her presence melting into the gloomy corners of the library as though she'd never been there at all.

"I can't find anything that fits the plant or the shadow." Orion huffed, dragging a hand across his forehead. "We've been here for hours and still nothing."

"I hear you," Elara said, shutting the ancient tome with a thud. "This library's like a haystack, and we're looking for a needle."

Orion scanned the library's high shelves with a furrowed brow. "We've read everything on these subjects we could find. And found nothing useful." He slammed the book shut on the table in front of him.

"We're missing something, then," Elara replied. "The answer has to be here. There has to be something here that can help us solve Professor Mistrial's murder and find Aegis of the Ancients."

With a sigh, Elara glanced around the mammoth room, her gaze falling on a thick gate in a corner that protected the books off limits to students. An idea, wild and daring, flashed in her mind.

"Hey, Orion," she said. "What if we, you know, tried looking in the restricted section?"

Orion raised an eyebrow. "You mean break the rules? Risk the wrath of the fire-breathing librarian? No thanks."

"Think about it," she said. "Whatever's going on at Charmcaster Academy is dangerous and secretive. Maybe the answers we need are tucked away with the forbidden books."

"Then that's where they'll stay," he said stubbornly.

Elara rolled her eyes. "Come on, Orion! Don't tell

me you're scared of a little rule breaking. Besides, this is for the greater good."

"Save it," Orion replied, looking a little uncomfortable. "I'm not thrilled about the idea of being on the wrong side of the headmistress."

"But imagine what we could uncover! Secrets that could help us figure out what's really going on here."

"No way." He crossed his arms and shook his head. "Girl, you are crazy. Anyone ever tell you that?"

"Sure a few times, but Orion, just think about it," Elara urged, her eyes wide, lashes fluttering. "There's so much we don't know about this place."

"But the rules, Elara" Orion began, clearly conflicted.

"Since when do rules get in the way of discovering the truth?" Elara shot back.

Orion sighed. "All right, you win. I can't believe I'm agreeing to this," he conceded, rubbing the back of his neck. "But if we get caught, you're the one explaining it to Headmistress Nightshade. And my parents."

"Deal." Elara said.

Orion gave a decisive nod. "Let's do it."

As they approached the entrance to the restricted alcove, Elara paused at the gated entrance.

Elara focused her wind magic on the gate. She

closed her eyes, channeling the power into her finger-tips. A gentle breeze grew, swirling and forming a small cyclone around the lock. The wind penetrated the lock, twisting and turning like an invisible key. A click echoed softly, and the gate opened slightly. Elara grinned at Orion.

The librarian's ever-watchful gaze could be their undoing if they didn't act carefully. Peering around the corner, she saw the librarian meticulously organizing a shelf, her plump figure and blue hair unmistakable even from this distance.

"Orion," she whispered. He turned toward her, a faint light glinting off his glasses. "You need to distract the librarian while I search the books."

"Me?" he asked hesitantly. "I'm not great at subterfuge."

"You got this," she said. "This might be our only chance to find out what happened to Professor Mistrial." She glanced into the restricted section. "Create a small scene, nothing too big. Just enough to keep the librarian's attention on you while I sneak inside."

"Fine," Orion agreed, taking a deep breath as if to steady his nerves. "I'll do my best."

"Thanks. Meet me in the empty classroom down the hall."

Orion took a deep breath, as if steeling himself,

before walking over to the librarian's desk. He had been trying to avoid the stern woman's gaze since they entered the library, but now he needed to attract her attention. On purpose.

"Excuse me," he said, wringing his hands nervously.

The librarian raised her eyebrows in response, but didn't lift her gaze from the book she was reading.

"Uh... I seem to have a bit of a problem," Orion continued, his voice slightly shaky.

The librarian sighed audibly, finally looking up from her book with an unimpressed expression. "Yes?"

On cue, Orion used his magic, focusing on a nearby potted plant. It started twitching and writhing as if taken by a wild wind. Leaves rustled, vines unfurled, and soon, the plant was stretching, reaching, knocking over a stack of books on a nearby table.

A gasp echoed through the library, and every eye—including the librarian's—turned toward the sudden chaos. As she shot out of her seat to investigate the scene, Orion glanced back at Elara, giving her a subtle nod. Now was her chance.

"Help me pick them up!" the librarian snapped, her yellow eyes narrowing as she surveyed the mess Orion created.

"Yes, ma'am," he muttered, his fingers working quickly to gather the scattered books.

With her pulse thundering, Elara cast one last glance at the main library, then slipped into the forbidden realm of the Elysium Archive, knowing that the answers they sought—and the consequences of their actions—lay just beyond the threshold. The silence pressed down on her as she scanned the shelves for any possible texts that might help them.

"Come on," she muttered under her breath, her fingertips grazing the cracked spines of ancient tomes.

Elara's hand landed on a dusty volume that caught her attention, its cover adorned with cryptic symbols and a dark, eerie aura surrounded it. She carefully pulled it from the shelf, feeling a shiver run down her spine as she held it in her hands.

As her fingers traced the worn pages, she felt a growing sense of urgency. "This has to be it," she said, her excitement building at the prospect of uncovering the truth.

She knew they didn't have much time before the librarian's suspicions would return, so she hastily tucked it under her arm and prepared to escape.

Clutching the ancient book tightly against her chest as she slipped back out of the alcove, Elara's breaths were shallow. She walked toward the exit, searching for any sign of the librarian's approach. Clutching the tome close to her chest, Elara knew she had to be swift and stealthy if they were going to make it out undetected.

"Almost there," she whispered to herself, as she reached the library's entrance.

Just as she was about to step into the hallway, the librarian glanced up, her eyes locking onto Elara's for a moment.

"Wait, what are you doing with that book?" she demanded, her plump body tensed with suspicion.

"Uh," Elara said. "I need it to study for an exam."

Orion looked at her and wrung his hands. On the floor sat a pile of books.

"Is that so?" The librarian's gaze narrowed. "Well, then. I suppose you should read it. But do not remove books from the library, young lady."

"Of course," Elara said, trying to sound as innocent and casual as possible. "I'll put it back when I'm finished."

"See that you do," the librarian warned before returning her attention to the books on the floor.

As she fled the library, Elara hurried along the corridor with the book to the empty classroom. A few minutes later, Orion entered and swung the door shut behind him, cutting off the chatter of students in the hallway. It was a small room, filled with mismatched desks and chairs, their wooden surfaces etched with the time-honored scribbles of bored students. Elara's breath caught as she looked around, suddenly aware of how eerily quiet it was.

"I did it. We did it!" At the last second, she remembered to whisper. Impatient to open the book, Elara sat it on one of the desks. "Now, let's see what this volume has for us."

She sat, and Orion took the seat opposite her. The thick leather cover seemed to sigh as she opened it, revealing pages that were yellowed and brittle with age. They exchanged an apprehensive glance, both keenly aware of the risk they'd taken to obtain it.

"Got a table of contents in that thing?" Orion asked.

"Good question," Elara replied, riffling through the book's first pages. She stopped at a list of chapters, her finger tracing down the page until it landed on a promising title: *Chapter 3, Dark Spells and Forbidden Magic*. "This could be what we're looking for."

"Dark spells?" Orion's voice wobbled a bit. "That sounds seriously creepy."

"I know, right?" Elara said. "But if we want to get to the bottom of Professor Mistrial's murder, we need to dig into the scary stuff." Her hand shook slightly as she turned to the grim chapter.

As they dove into the convoluted world of curses and hexes, the room seemed to grow tense, heavy with a sense of foreboding. It wasn't until they reached the chapter's last pages that they stumbled upon a chilling piece of information.

"Shadows' Grasp," Elara read out loud, goosebumps prickling her skin. "Just like the warning I got from my bedpost."

Orion read the text. "It lets the caster weaponized shadows, making them deadly tools to suffocate or crush their victims. And the best part? No fingerprints."

"Like the element of Umbrakinesis..." Elara said, her pulse jumping.

"Shadows." Orion said, his eyes going wide behind his glasses. "That ties in with the weird stillness we saw at the scene. It must have been this... Shadows' Grasp spell."

"I bet you're right." Elara said. "But who could've cast it? And why kill the professor?"

"Maybe there's more in the book," Orion offered, leaning in to study the pages.

Elara's eyes skimmed over the text, searching for a potential lead. Her heart pounded in her chest as she found a crucial passage. "Check this out," she said, her voice a low whisper. "The Shadows' Grasp is super advanced. Only a top tier Charmcaster could pull it off."

"Which means our killer has to be seriously skilled in magic," Orion deduced, his voice taut. "And probably someone high up, like a professor, definitely not a student."

"That's what I'm thinking," Elara said. "We need to find out who at the Charmcaster Academy could cast this spell. We can't let them get away with this. We've got to protect our school and our friends."

"Right," Orion agreed, his expression turning resolute. He jabbed a finger at the book. "So, this Shadows' Grasp spell needs a magic pro to work it. We need to compile a list of suspects with that level of skills."

"Where should we start?"

"Searching the teachers' resumes and backgrounds," he said. "Basically, we start with the Charmcaster Academy itself."

"Good idea," she replied, her face all hard-set and serious.

"What if someone notices our snooping and tries to stop us? Or the headmistress catches us, and we get into trouble?" Orion sat back. "I can't disappointment my family by getting kicked out of school."

"Then we'll just have to be careful," she replied, closing the book. "Now we need to put this tome back in the library without being caught by the librarian."

They carefully carried the ancient text and stealthily made their way back toward the library. Elara's heart raced as they navigated the corridors, avoiding any sign of the librarian. With a sigh of relief, they returned the book to its rightful place, silently celebrating their successful covert mission. Orion bid her farewell and headed to his dorm room, while Elara continued down the corridor toward her own room.

CHAPTER THIRTEEN

Students gathered in the courtyard after classes, some lounging on the grassy patches, others practicing spells under the supervision of their professors standing nearby. Among them was Orion, his heart pounding with courage and excitement. He adjusted his black-framed glasses and glanced around, eager for the tournament practice to begin.

Lush, verdant gardens surrounded the courtyard, and fluttering among the blossoms were small, winged creatures called whispervines, their laughter like the tinkling of tiny bells.

"All right, everyone!" boomed Professor Swiftwater, his dark brown skin and short black hair glistening under the warm sun. "Time to put your skills to the test! Remember, teamwork is essential in the Otherworld Triad Tournament!"

The enthusiastic students, including Elara, all shouted "OTT!" Orion noted the difference between him and his team.

As the students formed groups, Orion took a deep breath, focusing on the energy coursing through him. He could feel the life force of every plant in the courtyard beckoning him to join their dance. He stretched out his arms, palms facing the earth, and whispered an incantation. The ground trembled beneath his feet, and a moment later, vibrant green tendrils burst forth, twirling and twisting into intricate patterns. Gasps of awe echoed around him as the onlookers marveled at the display.

"Excellent work, Orion!" praised Professor Swiftwater, clapping his large hands together. "That's the skill that will make our school proud in the tournament!"

"Thanks, Professor," Orion replied, a blush creeping up his cheeks. He felt somewhat encouraged by the warm words of his mentor. A much-needed boost to his ego. He scanned the group of students to see if—by chance—Ivy saw.

"All right, everyone, let's keep practicing!" Professor Swiftwater called out, waving his arms with enthusiasm. "Push yourselves to your limits! Show me what you can do!"

The air filled with the sounds of incantations and magical bursts as Orion and his classmates honed their abilities. Orion was determined to prove himself, to show them he was more than just a shy boy with glasses. He continued to manipulate the surrounding plants, creating elaborate defenses and even surprising some of the older students with his prowess.

"Orion," said one of the senior students, panting after failing to break through his verdant barrier, "you're really something else."

"Thanks," Orion replied with a smile, his confidence growing like the very plants he commanded. He knew he had a long journey ahead, but with each successful spell, he felt closer to possibly winning the tournament.

Orion smiled as he watched a senior student struggle to penetrate his wall of thick vines and flower-laden branches. The boy attempted to force his way through, but Orion merely flicked his wrist, and the barrier tightened its grip.

"Admit it, you're stuck," Orion said cheekily, enjoying the moment.

"I give up!" the older student conceded, chuckling.

"You got me. I didn't expect such strong magic from someone your age."

"Neither did I," Orion admitted, allowing the barrier to dissolve back into the ground. He felt a newfound confidence coursing through him.

Within the courtyard, Orion noticed Professor Ember moving among the rarest of plants, her fingers hovering over the flora, careful not to touch. The shadows danced and twirled around her, coiling up stems and leaves, giving an euphoric quality to the space. Her eyes, sharp and focused, studied the enchanted vegetation as if searching for something hidden within their verdant confines. But as soon as she detected Orion watching her, she smiled a slow, scary grin and strolled inside the castle.

"That's it for today, everyone," the professor said in a booming voice. "Good job and we will reconvene next week."

The students gathered their belongings and headed back inside the castle.

"Orion! There you are," Elara called out.

Turning, Orion spotted Elara striding toward him from across the courtyard.

"Elara!" Orion couldn't hold back his grin. "You should've seen the stunt I just pulled off!"

"I saw, and you killed it," she said. "Done with

your session already? My coach bailed today, a nasty head cold."

"Bummer."

"Actually, I was hoping you'd help me get ready for the competition. I've got a plan, but we gotta keep it on the down-low," she said.

"Why does the sound of that seem as if you're gonna ask me to break more rules?" Orion queried, his eyebrows shooting up.

"Because you're my best friend and I need help. And we only train supervised," she said, snagging his hand. "Come with me."

As they slunk away toward the edge of the castle grounds, she let him in on her scheme. "We need a spot where no one can spy on us," she said, eyes darting around to make sure no one was tailing them. "A place where we can really push our limits without getting caught."

"Like Lumina Woods?" he suggested.

"Spot on," she agreed.

"This will get us expelled, Elara."

"Only if we get caught."

He threw up his hands. "Why can't I say no to you?"

"Because I'm pretty and keep your life exciting."

He laughed. "All true."

Venturing into the woods might be risky, but working his magic with Elara by his side gave him a shot of bravery.

"Okay. I can't believe I am saying this." Orion took off his glasses and pinched the bridge of his nose. "Let's sneak into the woods."

"First, we'll need a way over the walls," Elara elaborated as they neared the massive stone walls surrounding the castle. Elara would love to know more about the history of this place. Too bad they still don't have the moat, that would be outstanding.

"Consider it done," Orion said, a fire in his eyes.

"Well. Look at you all gung-ho today."

With a mischievous grin, he reached out towards the nearby ivy crawling up the wall. Concentrating his magic, he urged the vines to respond to his command. Slowly, the ivy tendrils reached out, entwining themselves and forming a sturdy ladder. Orion motioned for Elara to go first, her eyes wide with excitement. With nimble agility, she climbed the living ladder, gripping the vines tightly. Once she reached the top, she extended a hand to Orion. With a surge of grit, he grasped her hand, relying on his plant magic to carry him effortlessly over the high stone wall and down the other side.

They ran into the forest. Soon, Orion and Elara

were swallowed up by the green cocoon of the Lumina Woods. Giant trees, glittering with luminescent moss, bathed their path in an otherworldly glow. The smell of damp soil and floral perfume saturated the air, while the echo of owls and the sound of rustling leaves serenaded them.

"This place is insane," Orion murmured, his eyes bulging. He'd heard about the mystical beasts and supernatural plants of the Lumina Woods, but seeing it up close was a whole other level.

"Stay alert," warned Elara, her voice a mere whisper.

They found a forest clearing surrounded by trees and strange flora. Orion couldn't shake the feeling that unseen eyes were watching them. Every snap of a twig or rustle of underbrush made him tense up, ready to unleash his plant manipulation magic if needed.

"All right," said Elara. "I think we're far enough in. Let's practice."

"Agreed," said Orion.

They began by testing each other's abilities, with Orion manipulating the surrounding vegetation to create complex obstacles for Elara, who gracefully wove through them using her wind magic.

As they practiced, they gradually discovered how their skills complemented one another. Orion's ability to control plant life allowed him to create barriers and distractions, while Elara's wind magic could amplify his attacks and help them evade danger.

"Orion, watch this!" called Elara excitedly as she sent a gust of wind toward a cluster of leaves he had animated. The leaves swirled together at her command, forming a dense whirlwind that slammed into a nearby tree trunk with the force of a battering ram.

"Amazing!" Orion's eyes sparkled as he realized the potential their combined powers held. "Together, we'll be unstoppable."

As they continued to practice, Orion noticed how Elara's presence bolstered his confidence. Although he's been aware of his talent, he had often doubted himself when faced with pressure or adversity. But now, standing beside Elara, who he considered his best friend and ally, he felt more resilient and courageous than ever to win the tournament.

As Orion and Elara continued their practice session, the surrounding air felt heavier, as if charged with an unseen force. The phosphorescent moss that lit their path seemed to dim. The entire forest darkened.

"Orion," Elara whispered, her gaze darting around the darkening woods. "Do you feel that?"

He nodded, staring into the darkness. "Maybe we'd better head back now."

A deep, foreboding growl reverberated through the trees, shaking the very ground beneath them. An enormous, menacing beast emerged from the shadows, its hulking form bristling with thick matted fur. Its razor-sharp claws gleamed like daggers as it advanced toward them, and its glowing red eyes looked upon them with a fierce, predatory hunger. The air was so still, the same feeling they experienced in the vault. They could feel each thunderous step the beast took as it drew nearer. They needed to run. Now.

"Elara, it might attack. Get into a defensive position," Orion said, his voice barely rising above a nervous whisper. He balled his hands into fists, his veins pulsating with an expected rush of energy, ready to coax the surrounding foliage into defending them.

"We can handle this," she shot back, her lithe body poised like a coiled spring. Her wind magic danced around her fingers, standing by to hurl a tempest in an instant.

The surrounding air vibrated with tension as they braced for the beast's impending attack.

The creature pounced on them with a deafening roar, bringing its savage claws down toward Orion.

"Orion!" Elara cried out.

Elara thrusted her hands forward to send a powerful gust of wind at the creature. It struck the beast in its chest with enough force to at least make it stagger back.

The gale force blow was powerful enough to knock Orion's glasses off, but he managed to catch them just in time.

The beast stumbled back.

But only a second before regaining its footing.

Snarling.

Grunting.

Razor-sharp teeth were visible in this exhibition of rage.

With a wave of his hand, vines whipped up from the ground to wrap an unyielding restraint around the beast, but its reflexes were too quick and it rolled out of reach with an enraged roar.

"Keep it busy!" Orion yelled, his heart pounding as he frantically searched for some way to restrain the creature.

Seemingly aware of their fear and desperation...

The monster attacked.

Again.

A giant claw swiped at Elara. She jumped back, narrowly avoiding the beast. A beast determined to pierce any flesh in front of it.

Another pass of the deadly claws, but this swipe time it broke Elara's skin, sending a sharp jolt down her arm.

She jumped back and blasted the bear with tornado sized wind. Even with that, Elara could barely keep it away from her.

"Orion," Elara gasped out, her voice a rough blend of terror and resolve as she looked between the beast and her friend. Her eyes, usually so full of spirit, now mirrored the gravity of their situation. "We need to sync our powers. It's the only shot we have."

He returned her nod, forcing down the lump in his throat. "It's now or never," he responded, his voice thick with the taste of dread and excitement, steeling himself for the life-or-death dance they were about to undertake.

Before the creature charged at them once more, Orion and Elara acted in perfect unison. Orion raised one hand to the sky, his lips twitching in silent concentration as he called forth a tangle of thick vines from the earth. Elara mirrored his movements, her fingers flexing in complex patterns as she summoned a fierce straight-line wind. The air shot between the two teenaged heroes, picking up speed and intensity until it created a powerful force of nature.

They shouted their combined spell in unison, and

the wind seized the vines, intertwining them into an impenetrable net. The net flew through the air with incredible force, slamming into the rampaging beast and trapping it beneath its weight.

"Gotcha!" Orion cried out in triumph as the creature struggled against its bonds, roaring with frustration.

"Let's get out of here before it breaks free," Elara said, casting a worried glance at the thrashing creature.

"Agreed," Orion said. The adrenaline that had been fueling him faded, replaced by a throbbing pain and exhaustion.

Hurrying away, Orion felt a surge of pride well up within him as he reflected on their remarkable teamwork. Their ability to face a terrifying beast and emerge victorious was a testament to their trust and reliance on each other. With this newfound bond, they held the potential to become an overpowering force, ready to take on any challenge that awaited them in the upcoming tournament.

"Orion," Elara began, her voice slicing through the quiet hush that enveloped them. "Did we... did we just pull that off? I mean, together? Like we kicked some serious butt!"

A warmth, akin to a sunny summer day, fluttered

in Orion's chest. "I couldn't agree more," he responded, grinning.

She laughed, a light, bubbly sound. Though it was her normal tone, it seemed at odds with their recent encounter. Her eyes sparkled with contagious excitement. "You realize what this means for the tournament, right? If we can hold our own against a creature like that, imagine the edge we'll have against the others."

"Absolutely," Orion agreed, buoyed by their victory. The thought of triumphing in the tournament alongside Elara sent a thrilling shiver down his spine. A complete 180º from when his name was selected in the Great Hall that fateful day.

"But let's not get carried away," Elara added, her voice firm, pulling him back from his daydream. "We have more to do in preparation. And we can't lose sight of our other goal—solving the murder and finding the missing artifact."

"Got it. It all sounds simple enough, especially when you throw in any homework we'll surely be assigned." He said in a sarcastic tone. A way of speaking he hardly ever uses, but it seemed fitting. His burgeoning excitement was already tempered down by the reminder of their more somber mission. Going in the woods today was an unplanned side quest and now

Orion needed to get back on track. Despite the thrill of their recent victory, he understood they had a daunting challenge ahead. And he needed to be ready for whatever they found.

Nearing the castle grounds, Orion's mind raced with strategies for both the tournament and their investigation. He knew that together, they could face whatever challenges awaited them, be it a magical due. Or the tangled web of a murder mystery. Or even possibly a nocturnal nettle that could transport itself not only to this island, but into a vault.

CHAPTER FOURTEEN

L ife at Charmcaster Academy had an enchanting rhythm that was hard to resist. Days turned into weeks. Each sunrise brought a new magic-infused challenge for Elara. Lessons on controlling the elements, deciphering ancient scrolls, and countless hours practicing her wind magic became Elara's routine. But no matter how engrossed she was in her magical education, the shadows cast by Professor Mistral's murder lingered in her mind, a disturbing undercurrent beneath the rush of everyday school life.

Whenever she conjured a gust of wind or felt the caress of a zephyr on her face, she remembered the professor, who would never again experience the same. As her magical skills grew, so did her feeling of unease.

Whispers of the murder still echoed through the school's ancient corridors, a chilling reminder that even in a magical fortress like this, darkness could still find a way in.

Elara's footsteps echoed in the empty hall as she approached Professor Mistral's classroom. The door stood slightly ajar, and she hesitated for a moment before pushing it open with a soft creak. A faint layer of dust coated the desks, casting an eerie stillness over the room that had once pulsed with life.

"Professor Mistral, I'm so sorry and I'm going to help get you justice," Elara whispered to the room in the hopes that the late professor might hear her.

She could almost see the professor standing at the front of the class, her eyes sparkling as she demonstrated a complex weather spell. Shaking off the memory, Elara took a deep breath and crossed the threshold into the room.

The classroom lay undisturbed, as if waiting for its mistress to return. Elara felt a pang of sorrow for the woman who had so passionately shared her knowledge with them. Hoping to uncover the truth behind her murder, she made her way to the desk at the front of the room.

"Let's see what secrets you hold," she murmured, carefully lifting the lid of the wooden desk.

Neatly stacked papers greeted her, untouched since Mistral's last lecture. An uneasy feeling settled in the pit of her stomach as she began sifting through them.

"Nothing unusual here." Her fingers traced the neat handwriting on each page.

As she delved deeper into the contents of the desk, she noticed a small compartment. Her pulse quickened. She cautiously opened it to reveal a velvet-lined space where the key to the vault would fit perfectly.

"By the four winds!" Elara gasped, her heart pounding in her chest. "It's gone." The revelation sent a shiver down her spine, overwhelming her with implications she dared not consider.

"Focus, Elara," she told herself.

She needed to stay strong if she was going to solve this mystery and honor Mistral's memory. Closing the desk, she took one last look around the classroom, feeling as if an unseen presence watched her every move. The same feeling she got when she saw Professor Ember.

"Rest in peace, Professor," she whispered, her voice barely audible. Elara closed her eyes and tilted her head up to the ceiling for a moment of silence and reflection.

With a heavy heart, Elara stepped out of the room, the door clicking shut behind her. The missing key weighed heavily on her mind, and she knew she had to share her discovery with Orion.

Elara hurried along the corridor, the weight of her discovery making each step feel like a burden. The walls seemed to close in on her as she tried to process what she had found.

A shadowy figure rounded the corner and entered the corridor just ahead of Elara.

Professor Ember, a dark apparition swathed in her royal amethyst and black robes as usual. The figure glided toward Elara, Ember's presence a menacing force. Elara took a step back, suddenly afraid of the tall woman towering now over her.

"Ah, Elara," Professor Ember said, her dark robes swirling around her like an inky cloud. "A bit late for a visit to the classrooms, isn't it?"

"Oh, um, well," Elara stammered, trying to keep her tone neutral. "I... I just wanted to pay my respects to Professor Mistral."

"Understandable." Professor Ember's black eyes narrowed into thin blades of malice. "There is nothing more to be done for the dead. It would be prudent to focus on those who live instead, wouldn't you agree, Miss Silverwind?"

Elara furrowed her brow, unsure of how to respond. She weighed her words carefully. "Yes, Professor. Although there are still questions surrounding her death."

"Questions? I'm sure you're already aware of the missing Aegis of the Ancients." Professor Ember arched a single brow, a slow smirk curling across her face. "You'd be wise to walk away and forget all about it. To investigate such things can only bring chaos and despair; some secrets are better left in the shadows where they belong."

As Professor Ember spoke, her surrounding aura seemed to stir and pulse, adding a foreboding tone to her words. The darkness swirled around her like a living entity, ominous and gloomy. Elara's hands shook, and she took another step back.

"I was only curious about what happened to it," Elara said, trying to conceal the tremor in her voice.

"Hmmm," Professor Ember murmured. "Curiosity, Elara, is a double-edged sword. It can lead you to wisdom or be your ultimate downfall. Beware which edge you choose to wield."

"I don't understand." Elara's skin felt cold as if the shadows had sucked out all warmth and light. She looked at Ember with wide, fearful eyes. Her brave façade falling.

The corners of Ember's lips curved upward into a smirk, like a naughty child would possess. She leaned in closer to Elara. "Perhaps you'll comprehend this then," she whispered, her voice a low hiss in the now dark corridor. "Pry too much, dear Elara, and you might just uncover things that were better left hidden. Things... that could harm you or your friends."

With those intimidating words, Professor Ember stepped past her, her robes brushing Elara's arm in a cold sweep. She watched as the enigmatic professor disappeared into the adjacent hall. Her figure swallowed by her misty shadows.

Wow, she's creepy, Elara thought.

She continued toward the Elysium Archive, where she knew Orion would be studying. She needed to share her discoveries with him and discuss the implications of the missing key. With fear and excitement flowing through her, she inadvertently caused a twirling dervish to form around her. Blowing her hair and plaid skirt every which way.

Upon pushing the heavy, ornate doors of the library open, she spotted him. There was Orion, his frame bent over an imposingly large book, glasses perched on the edge of his nose, threatening to topple at any moment. The glow from enchanted candles, dancing to an enchanted rhythm, cast flickering shadows over his concentrated features as he furiously scribbled notes.

"Orion," Elara said, hurrying over to his table. "I've got something to tell you."

He blinked up at her, visibly surprised. "Elara, you okay? You look spooked. And your hair is a mess. Where were you?"

"You have questions. I have answers. So, listen. Ok, it's about Professor Mistral's murder," she began, her voice and breathing finally evening out to where Orion could understand her. "I was in her classroom snooping around for clues and the key to the artifact vault is not in Mistral's desk anymore. She told me that's where she kept it."

Orion dropped his pen, his eyes growing wide. "But the keeper always has it. You're saying...is its someone on the inside? Like someone on the faculty or a student?"

"I don't know. It could be," she said, shrugging. "And there's another thing. I bumped into Professor Ember, and she brought up Aegis of the Ancients. It was like she knew I was onto something."

Orion crinkled his nose. "Professor Ember gives me the creeps. What exactly did she tell you?"

"I think she sort of threatened me," Elara said, trying to recall the peculiar encounter.

"Wait..." He scratched his head. "One day, I saw Ember with a key, talking to another teacher in the hall. What if that was *the* key missing from Mistrial's desk?"

"Could be, but we'd have to be sure it's the same one before we point fingers at anyone."

"Looks like we've gotta dig deeper," Orion said resolutely. "We need to figure out the real story behind Mistral's death."

"Wanna snoop around in Professor Mistral's office next?" Elara proposed, her gaze steady.

"Count me in," Orion agreed, his resolve matching hers. "But for now, let's head to dinner. I'm starving."

Elara smiled. "You're always hungry."

"I'm a growing boy with mad plant skills," he teased. "So, yeah, I am always hungry."

Elara loved Orion's newfound confidence and enjoyed his sense of humor.

In the Great Hall, flickering candlelight cast shadows across the expressions of awe and laughter on the faces of the first-year students. Elara and Orion sat side by side at the long wooden table, lost in their thoughts as they picked at the remnants of the lavish meal laid out before them.

During dinner, Elara noticed that Professor Ember's table was silent in the sea of student chatter. Her keen brown-black eyes darted between the students, occasionally lingering on Orion and Elara till they turned away. The corners of her lips curled into a seemingly benign smile. She gracefully rose from her seat, her purple highlighted hair shimmering in the light, and she vanished like a wisp of a shadow.

When they were excused from dinner and told to go back to their dorm rooms, Elara and Orion went in the opposite direction.

As the night swallowed Charmcaster Academy, the moon threw a ghostly light on the cobbled pathways toward Professor Mistral's office. Stealthily, Elara and Orion wove their way through the vacant halls, their steps whispering against the ancient stones.

Muted torchlight danced on the imposing wood of Professor Mistral's office door, casting grotesque shadows on the finely wrought carvings of mythical beasts. Elara gave the door handle a tug, but it held firm.

"Now what do we do?" Elara murmured, concern etched on her face. "We can't unlock it."

"I've got an idea," Orion said. "Just watch my back."

"Can you really undo the lock? I don't know a spell for that."

"We're about to find out," he responded, a hint of resolve in his voice.

Orion reached into his pocket and drew out a tiny

green sprig, his personal magical companion, since he can't carry Seymore around. Concentrating, he whispered a word of power, imbuing the little plant with his magic. As if responding to an invisible command, the plant sprouted and stretched, its tendrils finding the minute cracks in the lock, prying and twisting until they heard a satisfying click. The door, once resistant, now swung open to their combined efforts, inviting them into the secrets it guarded.

The little plant shrank to its original size and retreated voluntarily back into Orion's pocket.

"Nice work." Elara smiled at Orion, admiration shining in her eyes. "Now let's see if we can find anything useful."

They slipped into the office, closing the door behind them as gently as possible. The room was filled with the scent of old books and lingering traces of sulfur from a magical energy spell. Orion and Elara moved carefully through the office, their heightened senses tuned in to detect anything out of the ordinary.

As they searched, the echo of Professor Ember's cryptic words haunted Elara's mind, urging her on in her quest for the truth behind Mistral's murder and the missing Aegis of the Ancients.

"First stop, her desk," Orion suggested.

"Good idea," Elara said, lighting a candle on the desk.

Elara's fingers trembled as she ignited a tiny flame on another candle, bringing some light to the shadowy room. The dancing flame reflected on Orion's glasses, who stood beside her.

While they searched the office and the desk, the air felt heavy with unanswered questions, and the faint scent of lavender still lingered in the room. Inhaling, it reminded Elara of Professor Mistrial's perfume.

"Elara, I think I found something!" Orion said excitedly, drawing her attention to a concealed drawer beneath the tabletop.

Elara leaned over to examine the hidden compartment. "Let's see what secrets it holds."

He carefully slid the drawer open, revealing a single piece of parchment folded neatly inside. Elara grasped the letter and unfolded it with trembling hands. The handwriting was unmistakably Professor Mistrial's, elegant and precise.

"Dear Headmistress," Elara read aloud, her voice wavering with emotion. "I am writing to express my deepest concern regarding Aegis of the Ancients. It has come to my attention that there are individuals within our esteemed academy who may plot to misuse the artifact for nefarious purposes. I cannot stand idly by and let this transpire..."

Orion listened intently, and Elara felt a chill as she continued reading.

"Consequently," she went on, "I have decided to remove Aegis of the Ancients from the upcoming Charmcaster Tournament. I understand that this decision may provoke significant controversy, but I believe it is necessary to protect our students and staff, and the sacred artifact itself..."

Elara paused, swallowing hard as she realized the implications of Mistral's words. She looked at Orion, whose face mirrored her own disbelief.

"Could this be why she was murdered?" Orion asked quietly, his voice cracking. "Someone didn't want her to remove the artifact as the winning prize?"

"Perhaps," Elara whispered, her mind reeling. "But by who? And where is the artifact now?"

Orion shook his head. "That's the mystery, but I feel like we're getting closer to uncovering the truth."

The two stared at each other in the dim candlelight, their resolve strengthened by the knowledge they had uncovered. They were no longer just searching for a missing artifact; they were seeking justice for Professor Mistral, and the truth behind her tragic demise.

Elara scanned the letter again, her blonde hair falling like a curtain around her face. The candlelight flickered, casting eerie shadows on the walls of Professor Mistral's office.

"Elara..."

She glanced up. "Yeah?"

Orion adjusted his glasses. "What's our next move?"

She looked up at him, and the strong resolve ignited inside her made Elara feel as though she could summon a tornado with a flick of her wrist.

"We don't stop until we find the truth, Orion," she replied firmly. "We owe that to Mistral. She was kind to us."

Orion swallowed hard, his Adam's apple bobbing. "You're right," he conceded, the faint candlelight high-lighting the hard set of his jaw. "Keep searching. Anything might be a clue."

A rustle of papers filled the silence as Elara's fingers sifted through the desk drawer's contents.

Orion's hand stilled hers, and she froze. "Hold on," he whispered, indicating a small, leather-bound journal tucked away under a pile of papers. "This looks interesting."

She took the journal, her hands carefully cradling the potentially critical piece of evidence. "Nice find,

Orion," she murmured, her fingers running along the worn leather before she slowly opened it.

"Is it Mistral's?" His voice was hushed, almost reverent.

"Yes," Elara confirmed, her eyes still devouring the lines. "It's her notes on magical artifacts, including Aegis of the Ancients."

He leaned closer. "Anything pointing toward a potential killer?"

"Perhaps," she replied noncommittally, continuing her perusal. "There are cryptic mentions of some faculty members."

"Ember?" His voice barely concealed his suspicion of the enigmatic professor.

"It's possible," Elara conceded, her gaze flickering back to Orion. "Why do you ask?"

He shrugged. "I just get bad vibes from that woman. I don't have any proof that she's involved, but I got a gut feeling that she is somehow."

"I do too, but we need solid evidence. No jumping to conclusions."

"Right," Orion said. "We continue our investigation, no matter where it leads."

"Exactly," she affirmed, finally tearing her eyes away from the journal to look at him. "Together, we will ensure justice for Professor Mistral."

In the swirling breeze of the candlelit room, Elara's eyes shimmered with the power of a gusty gale, mirroring the dancing flames. The weight of their mission bore down on her shoulders like the fear of an incoming storm. But with Orion by her side, she felt a surge of bravery course through her. Together, they would navigate the intricate web of mysteries that gripped Charmcaster Academy, unmasking the assailant responsible for the heinous murder that had sent shockwaves through their cherished school.

CHAPTER FIFTEEN

After his last class of the day, Orion found himself standing in the austere confines of Headmistress Nightshade's office. Tasked by the librarian to return an ancient text from the Elysium Archive to the headmistress's personal collection, he took in the room's daunting grandeur. Ornate shelves held esoteric artifacts and weathered scrolls towered overhead, the soft flicker of magic-lit lanterns casting shifting shadows.

The air held a tangible sense of authority and wisdom, further amplified by the silence that seeped into every corner. The headmistress's towering desk stood at the far end, piles of files and ancient tomes atop its polished surface.

Treading lightly, Orion carefully placed the text on the edge of the desk.

As he was about to exit, a particular shelf caught his eye. It held staff records, a thorough history of academic contributions by the professors of Charmcaster Academy. Among these was an intriguing, aged dossier labeled: *Professor Ember*.

Curiosity piqued, Orion pulled the folder from its place, scanning the contents under the low glow of the nearby lantern. The contents revealed a side of Professor Ember he'd never suspected—detailed accounts of her past involvement with Shadows' Grasp.

"Ah-ha!" Orion whispered.

His heartbeat quickened as he sifted through the brittle pages, each holding detailed notes about this obscure dark magic.

Surprised by this revelation, Orion knew Elara needed to see this. Pocketing the dossier with a quick glance around to ensure he was still alone before leaving the headmistress's office.

Walking along the bustling corridor of Charmcaster Academy, he couldn't wait to tell Elara. He tried to walk as fast as possible toward Elara's dorm room without looking too suspicious.

A flock of scrollbirds flapped through the high

archways, carrying envelopes in their beaks, serving as the academy's unique postal service. Orion grinned as he watched them swoop and swerve with precision, delivering letters to students.

Orion hesitated for a moment outside Elara's door, his hand poised to knock. The dossier felt heavier than ever, its weight a physical manifestation of the dark secrets it contained. He took a deep breath and knocked firmly.

"Come in," Elara said from within the room.

Orion pushed open the door, the hinges creaking their protest as he stepped inside.

"Hey, Orion!" Elara greeted him, her attention instantly pulled to the weathered dossier clutched in his hands. "What've you got there?"

Orion shuffled uncomfortably, his gaze darting around the room. Satisfied they were alone, he dropped his voice. "It's about Ember," he began, his words crisp and serious. "I ran into something interesting in the headmistress's office. It's a record of her researching, and even mastering, the Shadows' Grasp spell."

Elara's eyebrows shot up, her words nearly a whisper, "Are you serious?" She ran a hand through her platinum hair, agitated. "That means she uses…"

"Dark magic," Orion finished for her, the words hanging heavily in the air.

As he spoke, a gust of wind whistled through the room, rustling papers on Elara's desk, as if mirroring the storm of thoughts churning within her.

"Let's sit," Elara said, her voice steady despite the news. She motioned toward a chair by the window. "We need to go over this dossier together and figure out what it means."

As they pored over the dossier, piecing together Ember's past research with involvement with the Shadows' Grasp. A chilling realization took shape. The only person known to have extensive knowledge about the Shadows' Grasp within Charmcaster Academy was none other than Professor Ember herself.

"Orion," Elara said, her voice threaded with worry. "The Shadows' Grasp isn't just any spell. It's lethal and leaves no trace of being cast. If Ember's been meddling with it... she could have used it on Mistral."

Orion's grip tightened around the dossier, his gaze steady on Elara. "You're right, but we can't just go accusing her without solid proof."

Elara nodded. "And we've got to play it smart, lie low. We don't want Ember catching wind of our suspicions." Her hand absentmindedly toyed with her wind-charmed pendant, a symbol of her focus.

"Okay. Let's go get some proof," Orion said, standing up. "We should start by talking with the other teachers about Ember. See what they know about her and that dangerous spell?"

"Good thinking," she agreed.

Orion and Elara left her dorm room, their determination cutting through the chill of the hallway. Together, they ventured over to the academy's main building.

"Let's talk with Professor Stonebrook. He might be wrapping up his Earth Magic class about now." Orion adjusted his glasses, turning down the long corridor lined with portraits of previous headmasters.

As they reached the Earth Magic classroom, the door opened to reveal the sturdy figure of Professor Stonebrook. His square jaw was set in stern lines, his dark-brown hair neatly combed. He looked up from examining a set of crystals, meeting their gaze with an arched eyebrow.

"Orion, Elara, what brings you here?" Professor Stonebrook asked, looking up from his crystal arrangement. His dark green attire harmonized with his surroundings. He gestured for them to take a seat as he leaned back in the chair.

Orion and Elara sat in the stiff wooden chairs facing him.

"We were hoping you might help us understand something about Shadows' Grasp," Orion said, hoping his voice didn't sound as nervous as he felt.

The professor's brow furrowed as he steepled his hands thoughtfully, his copper ring glinting in the dim light of the room. "That's a treacherous invocation," he responded, caution edging his voice. "Not one for students to dabble with. Why the curiosity?"

Elara shifted in her seat, her nervous fingers finding the pocket of her uniform. "We wondered if any of your fellow professors studied it? Now or in the past, maybe?" Elara asked, hoping for a straightforward answer.

The professor stroked his chin thoughtfully and settled back in his chair. "To the best of my knowledge, none. But..." His momentary hesitation preceded his next words. "Professor Ember did show a particular interest in the dark arts when she joined the school."

Orion leaned forward, eyes flashing with interest. "When was that?"

"They hired her during summer break. She replaced a professor on maternity leave. So basically, she's been here a little longer than you first year students." Stonebrook replied, his gaze growing distant. "Ember's quite the recluse. Doesn't mingle much with any of us. At first, I thought she was shy but now that it has been a few months...well, I can't speak for my fellow professors but a few of us, myself included, find her a bit odd. And not in the funny, artsy way."

Elara tucked an errant blonde hair behind her ear. "Ever noticed her acting...strange?" she asked, trying to avoid sounding too suspicious.

The professor's eyes narrowed as he glanced between them both. "How do you mean?"

"Perhaps out of character," Orion said as he drummed his fingertips on the armrest of his chair. "A change in routine, perhaps? Or has she avoided any professors or students in particular?"

The professor paused, a thoughtful expression settling on his face. "She's been a bit more secretive lately. Spending a lot of time in her office, even after school hours."

With each word spoken, Orion felt anxious over this potential connection to their suspicion.

"Interesting." Orion straightened in his chair. "We appreciate your insight, Professor."

"Well, just be careful with your curiosity," Stonebrook said solemnly. "Dark magic and those who use it, are not to be trifled with."

"Of course, Professor," Elara agreed quickly as she rose to her feet. "We'll keep that in mind."

The pair navigated the winding corridors of the academy, eventually finding themselves on the outskirts of the Water Magic training grounds outside the academy but safely within the grounds of the property. Here, students practiced forming whirlpools and manipulating water currents under the attentive guidance of Professor Swiftwater. The burly man, known for his charismatic and lively personality, stood tall in his turquoise attire, a stark contrast to his dark skin. His short black hair glistened in the sunlight as he watched his students with a keen eye.

Approaching him, Orion cleared his throat to catch the professor's attention. "Excuse me, Professor Swiftwater?" Orion raised his voice to be heard above the lively chatter and splashing water.

Swiftwater turned, his eyes crinkling with a friendly smile as he recognized them. "Orion, Elara! What brings you to my watery wonderland?"

"We have some questions," Orion said. "About Professor Ember."

Swiftwater's smile instantly disappeared, his jovial demeanor dimming upon hearing her name. "Ah, Ember. Quite the enigma, isn't she?" He shrugged, his muscular arms rippling with the movement. "Let's step inside for a moment."

The three of them ventured into the castle and stood in a foyer facing the water grounds.

"So, what did you want to know?" Professor Swiftwater asked.

Elara cleared her throat. "Just, um... what's she like?"

Swiftwater looked around the room, taking in the ancient books that lined the walls and the flickering candles casting shadows along the ceiling. "Keeps to herself mostly. And she has a fierce intensity about her. But then, don't we all have our quirks? Why the sudden interest?"

"We've heard about her expertise in the dark arts." Elara tugged at the collar of her crisp white shirt under her school uniform and stepped forward into a shaft of sunlight streaming through a stained-glass window. "Particularly, her research on the Shadows' Grasp spell."

"That's not an incantation anyone should trifle with..." His words trailed off as the professor noticed their grave expressions and he frowned slightly, tapping his finger on his chin. "As for Ember, I can't say much about her interests. We don't really discuss our academic pursuits."

Orion felt a tinge of disappointment at the vague response, but he understood. As much as they needed information, it wouldn't do to have rumors flying around the school. The students needed to trust their teachers, after all.

Orion stepped forward and met the professor's gaze. "Have you noticed anything unusual about her recently?"

"Well," Stonebrook finally broke the silence, his voice thoughtful, "now that you mention it, there's been a certain... restlessness about her. But we all have our own share of troubles. The Academy can be quite demanding and this is only her first year here." A flicker of hesitation appeared in the professor's eyes. Stonebrook's normally stoic face seemed to wrestle with some unspoken thought. "Professor Ember's been a bit reclusive lately. More than usual, I mean. Mostly cooped up in her office, even during leisure hours."

Stonebrook's words gave him pause. A restlessness? What could that mean? Was it a sign of guilt, or just the normal stress of teaching?

"Actually, Professor Swiftwater," Orion said, his fingers trembling as he adjust his glasses, the quiet clinking of the frames carrying throughout the quiet room. "There's something else we wanted to ask you about."

Swiftwater eyed them from below his shaggy eyebrows. "Go on."

Orion leaned closer and spoke in a hushed tone. "It's about the recent theft at the school, the artifact, Aegis of the Ancients, from the vault."

The professor crossed his arms, gazing out of the window to view the misty lawn of the castle. He sighed heavily. "Aye, a tragedy indeed," Swiftwater muttered. "It's not every day you hear of an ancient artifact going missing in these hallowed halls."

"That's just it." Elara said. "We were wondering if you'd noticed anything strange the day it was stolen. Anything out of the ordinary? Maybe something about Professor Ember?"

Swiftwater shook his head slowly. "Can't say I did, kids. I was here on the grounds all day and don't see Ember at all..." He paused and rubbed his chin and pursed his lips. "But, now that I think of it, I do recall her being more absent than usual around that time."

In the silent hall, they heard a distant owl hoot through an open window. It must be a Moonseer, Orion thought.

"That fits with what we've been hearing," Orion said, sharing a quick glance with Elara. The pieces were slowly forming a picture, but they needed more. "Thanks for your help, Professor Swiftwater."

The burly man waved a dismissive hand. "You're welcome. And while curiosity is a great thing, caution is greater. Be careful, you two."

"Thanks, Professor Swiftwater," Elara said, offering the man a grateful smile.

"Stay safe, you two." Swiftwater's jovial demeanor resurfaced as he headed back to his class outside.

Orion and Elara stood in the foyer for a moment.

"Where to next?" Elara asked.

"Professor Frostwood. She's probably *chilling* in her office. I heard she's as cold as ice, but maybe she'll thaw out for us," Orion said, laughing at his own joke.

Elara rolled her eyes, her smile matching his own. "Come on."

In another section of the school, there were floating orbs of light that replaced the need for torches, their soft glow eerily illuminating the beautiful stonework and archaic tapestries lining the walls. Books filled the air with the rustling of levitating pages, the subtle whispers of mischievous ghosts, and an underlying scent of magical plants.

Orion and Elara reached a part of the castle where the antechambers were coated with a thin sheen of frost, a telltale sign they were approaching the office of Professor Frostwood. Before them stood a massive door carved with intricate images of winter landscapes.

Taking a deep breath, Orion knocked on the door, the sound echoing softly in the chilled air.

"Enter!" a female voiced bellowed.

They found Professor Frostwood behind her desk, a vision of arctic beauty. She decorated the room in hues of white and silver, complementing her frosty appearance. Shimmering icicles hung from the ceiling, enchanted snowflakes twirled in mid-air, and a crackling fireplace emitted a cozy warmth despite the icy ambiance. It was like stepping into a magical snow globe.

She sat behind a huge white desk, her platinum hair and crystal blue eyes seemed to sparkle under the cool, white glow of the illuminated snowflakes that floated lazily around the ceiling. Her silvery robes rustled softly as she graded papers on her desk.

"Hi, Professor Frostwood," Elara said, politely knocking on the door that was partially open.

The professor looked up from her parchment-covered desk, her icy blue eyes meeting their gaze. "Yes?"

Since they weren't in any of Professor Frostwood's classes yet, Elara introduced herself and Orion. "I'm Elara and this is Orion. We're first-year students, and we wanted to speak with you if you have a minute, please?"

"Sure. What can I do for you, young Charmcasters?" Professor Frostwood asked, setting the pen she was holding on the desk.

"We've been trying to learn more about the academy's history," Orion said, gesturing toward a wall adorned with portraits of past faculty. "And we were curious about Aegis of the Ancients artifact that was stolen."

Professor Frostwood's brow furrowed, her cool demeanor momentarily disturbed. "The artifact's disappearance is quite troubling. It vanished shortly after Professor Mistrial passed away."

"That's quite a coincidence, isn't it?" Orion said, trying to not sound overly invested.

"Perhaps, but coincidence isn't the same as causation," Frostwood replied, her gaze penetrating. "Why the sudden interest in the artifact? Most first-year students aren't aware of the artifacts."

Orion's hand clenched into a fist, his nails digging into his palm. Was Frostwood onto them? He dared a glance at Elara, who seemed to be as nervous as he was.

"Oh, no particular reason, just... curiosity, you know." Elara played with the hem of her sweater vest, her eyes downcast.

A small puff of lavender-colored smoke emerged from one of the ink pots on Professor Frostwood's desk. It materialized into a tiny, lithe dragon, no bigger than a hummingbird. It fluttered its iridescent wings before settling on the professor's shoulder, its miniature fire puffs setting the professor's quill aflame. The professor merely raised an eyebrow and extinguished the fire with a dismissive wave of her hand.

"Oh, don't mind Flicker, he's quite mischievous," Professor Frostwood snickered. "Likes to play with fire, even if it's at my expense."

Elara giggled, her eyes sparkling at the sight of the little dragon. "He's quite adorable, though."

"Hardly the word I'd use," the professor muttered, retrieving the now charred quill. "Now, what is it you two want?"

Elara finally straightened her spine and raised her eyes to meet the professor's. "Professor, it's just that... well, we've noticed some strange things happening lately. Around, involving, Professor Ember."

Orion quickly added, "And it's not just us. Others have noticed it too."

There was a pause in which Professor Frostwood studied them, her expression unreadable.

Finally, Orion broke the silence. "We heard Professor Ember's quite an expert in her field of shadow magic and studies of the dark arts. Is that true?"

Frostwood's gaze sharpened. "Yes, I've heard that, too," she responded carefully. "Ember is indeed quite knowledgeable."

A chill ran down Orion's spine as he met Frostwood's gaze. He felt a mix of admiration and unease, aware that her sharp intuition might make her a formidable ally or a challenging obstacle to their investigation. He felt like an amateur spellcaster trying to outwit a master Charmcaster, and he hoped his act wasn't as transparent as it felt.

"She's rather private, though, isn't she?" Orion said, trying to keep the conversation casual and on track. "Must be difficult getting to know her."

"Yes," Frostwood said, her eyes narrowing ever so slightly, a smirk playing on her lips as if she caught a whisper of their hidden intentions. "She does prefer her solitude. But then, many of us here do."

Orion swallowed a sudden lump in his throat. Was Frostwood onto them? Did she suspect their true intentions? He needed to tread carefully or risk exposing their covert investigation.

"But surely she interacts with other professors, right?" Elara pushed gently, her fingers absentmindedly twirling a strand of hair. "How does she get along with them?"

Frostwood leaned back in her chair, her hand

gracefully stroking her chin as she considered how to answer. "She's professional, mostly," she replied. "Though I do sense that she might be hiding something."

A jolt of adrenaline shot through Orion. Their hunch was right. They weren't alone in their suspicions about Ember. He exchanged a quick look with Elara, his heart pounding in his chest.

"Then again, aren't we all hiding something?" Frostwood added, her voice echoing in the cool, hushed silence of her office, sending chills down Orion's spine. He suddenly felt the temperature in the room drop a few degrees. "Now, I must get back to grading these papers. Is there anything else?"

"About Professor Mistrial..." Orion said, pushing up his black-framed glasses.

A flicker of sorrow crossed Professor Frostwood's frosty countenance. "A tragic loss for our institution," she said, her voice more delicate than they had heard before. "Such a valued faculty member."

Swallowing hard, Elara said quietly, "We... we were the ones who found her. In the artifact vault."

The icy professor stilled, her gaze fixated on them. "A grave experience for you both. As you must know, the vault houses several artifacts with potent magic. Mishandling can lead to... unfortunate incidents. They deemed Mistral's death an accidental mishap involving an artifact."

Orion shifted his weight. "Has there been other accidents like this before, Professor?"

"Well..." The snowy-haired professor considered the question. "Mishaps have occurred," she confessed. "But none so disastrous as to cause the loss of life. However, Aegis of the Ancients must not fall into the wrong hands. Should dark magic misuse or corrupt it, it could bring devastation upon all realms."

At Professor Frostwood's warning, a chill skated down Orion's spine.

"Do you think Professor Mistrial had anything to do with the missing Aegis of the Ancients, by any chance?" Elara asked, trying to keep her voice steady.

Frostwood looked sharply at them. "Mistrial was a woman of integrity. I have no reason to believe she had any unsavory intentions."

Flushing slightly, Elara quickly clarified. "We didn't mean to imply anything wrong, Professor. It's just been hard to wrap our heads around everything. The unsettling events at the academy..."

"Yes, they've left a bitter chill," Frostwood agreed, her gaze distant. "Mistrial's demise and the artifact's disappearance have left a slew of unanswered questions."

"Professor," Orion ventured, his voice tremulous. "Do you think there's a chance that someone inside the academy might be involved? Another professor, perhaps?"

Her lips thinned, though her demeanor was as cool as before. "It's a disturbing thought. However, without tangible evidence of foul play, it remains a heartbreaking accident."

"Thank you for your time, Professor Frostwood," Elara said, giving the ice queen a warm smile.

"Good day, children," the professor said, and she went back to grading papers.

As they left Frostwood's office, Orion could still feel her frosty gaze on them.

"I can't shake off the feeling that they all know more than they're letting on," Orion said, rubbing his forehead.

Elara nodded in agreement. "Especially Frostwood. Did you notice how her demeanor changed when we brought up Ember?"

"Yeah, it was subtle, but noticeable," Orion agreed. "And Stonebrook, too, seemed to hesitate when talking about Ember's interests."

"Swiftwater brushed it off, though," Elara pointed out. "But it could just be his nature."

"Right," Orion murmured, deep in thought.

"Either way, we're on the right track, Elara. We just need to keep investigating."

"And stay off Ember's radar," Elara added.

Orion and Elara returned to their rooms, more questions in their minds than answers. The conversation with each professor was inconclusive, but their resolve had solidified. They would uncover the truth and expose the murderer.

CHAPTER SIXTEEN

The next day, after their encounters with the three professors, Elara and Orion found themselves standing in the castle foyer. An ethereal glow from the rising sun filtered in through the stained-glass windows, splashing vibrant colors onto the ancient stone floors. Elara glanced at the oversized bronze sundial at the center of the academy's front entrance, an ancient artifact said to be capable of tracking not just earthly time but the ebb and flow of magic itself, casting shimmering lights that made the solid stone look like it was shifting and rippling.

"I think it's time we speak with Professor Ember and straighten things out. Get the truth," Elara said, her voice barely above a whisper. "We already know that Ember has extensively studied ancient and forgotten spells, including the Shadows' Grasp."

She knew they were taking a risk by confronting her, but they needed answers and if facing Ember was the only way to get them, then so be it.

"Are you sure about this?" Orion asked, lifting the strap of his backpack higher on his shoulder.

Elara shrugged, trying to shake off the nerves that had been gnawing at her since she woke up. "Do we really have another choice? We can't ignore Professor Ember as the potential killer and thief. And we won't know for sure unless we talk to her."

Orion raised an eyebrow. "So she's guilty until proven innocent?"

She shrugged. "In a case like this, I'd rather be safe than sorry. Wouldn't you?"

He nodded. "I have this weird feeling that she'll be proud of herself and want someone else to know," Orion said. "Like to show off, you know?"

"Why don't we see if we can find something that ties her to Mistrial's death? We can visit her office and just take a quick look around."

Their voices bounced off the walls, swallowed up by the enchanted silence spell that always lingered in the entrance hall, making it seem like they were inside a vast, empty cavern.

"You're right," he said. "And if Ember's guilty, then we can't let her get away with what she's done."

Drifting down from a hidden vent in the ceiling, a tiny creature, no bigger than a fairy, appeared with a mischievous twinkle in its yellow eyes. It flitted around the room, leaving a trail of sparkling dust in its wake.

Elara's eyes widened in awe. "Is that a pixie sparkler?"

Orion followed her gaze, a smile tugging at his lips. "Yeah, it is. Little guy must've slipped through the fairy door upstairs. They're notorious eavesdroppers."

Elara beamed. "I love this school! Only at Charm-caster Academy would we consider a spying pixie normal."

The pixie flew over Elara's head and doused her with a ton of pixie dust, coating her blonde hair like a vibrant explosion of confetti.

Elara sputtered, shaking her head to rid herself of the excess sparkles. "Just great. I've been glitter bombed!"

Orion couldn't contain his laughter. His shoulders shook. "Don't worry, Elara." He reached out to gently brush the sparkles from Elara's hair. "You've just got a touch of pixie glam," he teased.

Elara swatted at the lingering sparkles, feigning

exasperation. "Well, I hope it goes well with my uniform."

Orion grinned wider. "You might become the latest fashion trend at Charmcaster Academy."

Elara rolled her eyes. "Well, I do rock this pixie-chic look."

They both burst into laughter, the sound blending with the enchanting atmosphere of the castle foyer. It was moments like these that made her grateful for the magical world she was a part of.

With a final loop and a flick of its tiny wings, the pixie sparkler dove out through an open window, leaving behind an aura of light and a sprinkling of stardust that danced in the air before gently settling down.

Sobering, the two friends took a moment to gather their courage, exchanged a plucky glance, and started to navigate the labyrinthine corridors. The castle was just waking, the gargoyles that lined the halls grumbling and stretching, their stone bodies groaning with effort.

Winding their way through the school, their footsteps echoed on the stone floor. The classrooms and offices they passed were mostly empty, the magical torches lining the walls casting flickering light across their faces. They halted at a heavy wood door that bore the engraved plaque: *Professor Ember*.

Inhaling deeply, Elara raised her hand and rapped her knuckles against the polished mahogany door of Professor Ember's office. The heavy silence that followed felt loaded with anticipation, making her heart pound in her chest.

Hesitantly, she reached out to the cool brass handle and gave it a twist, but it wouldn't budge. Of course, Ember had locked her office. Elara glanced at Orion, his encouraging nod giving her the push she needed.

Her fingers twitched in a specific pattern, and she whispered a soft incantation under her breath, a trace of ethereal blue light flitting from her fingertips. But the door remained stubbornly shut. The lock was enchanted.

"Looks like it's going to be trickier," Elara said, a determined gleam in her eyes. "Stand back, Orion."

She adjusted her stance to focus on her magical energy. Her incantation grew louder, more commanding, and the blue light flared brighter. For a moment, it seemed like the door would stand resolutely.

But then, with an almost inaudible click, the lock gave way.

Elara breathed out a sigh of relief. "I did it!" She caught herself right before she was about to yell out with excitement that Elara remembered this was a covert operation. She realized that wind magic was more her thing than perfecting her skills of breaking and entering.

"Nice work, Elara," he said. "Now let's see what Ember is hiding."

They cautiously—and quietly -stepped inside.

Professor Ember's office was submerged in a state of permanent twilight, an eerie semi-darkness that clung to the corners and crept along the floorboards. Elara's skin prickled in the chill as she noticed the high, vaulted shelves were crammed with time-ravaged books. Their leathery covers groaned with cryptic secrets, as if their faded pages were whispering tales of sorcery and curses from centuries past.

Walking further into the chamber, they navigated past a large mahogany desk that looked like a relic from a bygone era. It was an island of clutter in the room's shadowy tranquility, strewn with vellum scrolls, blackened inkwells, and a motley array of peculiar trinkets and curiosities. The objects buzzed with an inherent magical aura that filled the room with an otherworldly hum, while the scents of ink and ancient parchment mingled with an underlying trace of something far older and more ominous.

A sleek silver quill danced effortlessly across a document on the desk, weaving its own magical tale in elegant strokes. It moved with a grace all its own, as if guided by an invisible hand. Ink flowed from its feathery tip, leaving behind glistening trails that shimmered briefly before setting in place.

"Maybe she's out," Orion said, scanning the room for any sign of the enigmatic professor and setting his backpack down near the desk. "Does she have a class this morning?"

"I'm not sure," Elara replied. "Wherever she is, she won't like that we broke into her office."

Orion shrugged, a mischievous glint in his eyes. "Well, if we get caught, we can always tell her we were just admiring her wicked sense of interior decorating."

Elara giggled, nervously scanning the room once more. "Very funny, Orion. But remember, we're not here for a design critique. Let's just look around for clues and get out."

Rummaging through Ember's disorderly desk stirred a twinge of remorse in Elara. It felt wrong to pry into the professor's personal space, but the disturbing image of Mistrial's cold, lifeless body swiftly drowned out her guilt. They needed to find her killer, and this was their best lead.

"Got something," Elara murmured, waving a scrap of paper in her hand. It was Ember's schedule. "According to this, she should be in the middle of a lecture."

Orion nodded. "Then we're safe to poke around."

Suddenly, a flicker in the corner of the room caught Elara's attention. A shadow twisted and writhed on the wall, taking on an unsettlingly human-like shape. Orion must've noticed it too, because he froze mid-search, his eyes wide with apprehension.

Before they could react, the shadow formed into a menacing creature, its silhouette indistinct yet oddly terrifying. It seemed to survey the room, its formless head leaning forward at the sight of the intruders.

Without a sound, it slithered away, disappearing into the inky darkness of the room. Its silent departure left a lingering chill in the air, a dreadful sign that they were no longer alone in their secret mission.

Orion gulped audibly, turning to Elara with wide eyes. "You think it went to tell Ember?"

"Probably. There are eyes everywhere in this building, even on walls." Elara whispered back, her voice barely a whisper. "We need to hurry."

Elara's eyes scoured the room, filled with an uncanny array of shadowy corners and towering shelves crammed with weathered books and curios. Something drew her attention to a faded tapestry partially covering an indentation in the stone wall. With a cautious glance at Orion, who was elbow-deep in an odd cabinet filled with strangely shaped bottles, Elara lifted the heavy fabric.

Underneath lay a daunting metal safe, integrated so flawlessly into the stone wall that it seemed a part of it. Its elaborate lock was a labyrinth of rotating wheels and strange symbols, a defiant guardian to the treasures within.

Orion, catching her eye, joined her. A quick, shared look confirmed their suspicions—this had to be where Professor Ember hid her most valued possessions. The casual clutter of her office was a mere smokescreen.

Orion, swallowing nervously, reached out a hand toward the lock. Elara watched as he traced the symbols on the lock, his face taut with concentration. After a long moment, he attempted to rotate the wheels, his fingers trembling slightly. There was a click, but the door remained stubbornly closed.

His shoulders slumped in disappointment. "I guess it's not that easy," he said, rubbing the back of his neck. "You wanna try?"

Elara nodded and stepped forward. She closed her eyes, the air around her fingers conjuring up a wind gust as she channeled her wind magic. She focused, visualizing the lock mechanisms moving and aligning in the correct order. As she opened her eyes, she pointed her hand towards the safe, guiding the invisible currents towards the stubborn lock. There was a moment of expectation as the air whirled around the lock, but then it died down without the needed *click*. Opening the safe was beyond her abilities. She sighed, frustration flickering in her eyes.

"Guess wind magic doesn't work on everything," she said, stepping back with a light shrug. Elara sighed.

Orion's eyes brightened. "Let me try something else."

Raising his hand, he whispered an incantation, and a soft green glow developed on his fingertips. Small tendrils of vine sprung forth, intertwining and pressing against the intricate lock, trying to comprehend its complex language. There was a moment of anticipation before a soft click sounded again, this time followed by the groaning creak of the safe door opening. The two interlopers both let out a sigh of relief. The hard part was done. Hopefully, it gets easier from here. Hopefully.

Inside, among a collection of oddities, lay a brilliantly crafted artifact that resembled a golden trophy and an intricately carved key.

"Orion, check this out," Elara whispered, pointing toward the artifact and the key.

Orion, his eyes wide, picked up the key. "I recognize this. It's an identical key to the one Ember was carrying the other day. This is the vault key!"

"And it is the perfect shape I found in Mistral's office."

Elara looked at the artifact, her heart pounding in her chest. "And this is the Aegis of the Ancients artifact from the vault. Which means we connected Ember to Mistral's death. If not as the killer, then certainly as the thief."

"If Ember had the key, then she had access to the vault." Orion mused, his fingers brushing over the smooth metal. "She has to be the murderer, too."

Elara bit her lip, her thoughts churning. They had evidence, yes, but it was circumstantial at best. Mere coincidence. She looked at Orion. His brows were slightly furrowed, his eyes focused and intense.

"We need to leave, Orion, like right now," she whispered. "Before we're discovered. We need to bring this to Headmistress Nightshade's attention. It might not pin Ember as Mistral's killer, but it's something."

Orion nodded, quickly placing the artifact and key into his backpack. "You're right. Let's move. We can't afford to get caught here."

Elara noticed that Orion's fingers trembled on the handle of his backpack, just as she felt the air grow cold in front of them.

The office door exploded open and banged against the stone wall with a suddenness that caused a gasping, icy gust to blow through the room. Framed in the menacing gloom of the hallway, Professor Ember loomed, her form commanding and ominous. Her height might have been average, but under the murky shadows cast by the torchlight, she seemed larger, more imposing. Her slender figure crackled with an eerie aura, amplifying the unease that writhed through the dimly lit room. Her presence, dark and powerful, swallowed the room's warmth, replacing it with a bone-chilling temperature drop.

Elara froze in her tracks, her breath hitching in her throat. She felt like a deer caught in headlights as she whirled around to face the office door. Elara's heart pounded wildly in her chest, its frantic rhythm echoing in her ears. Orion quickly moved to stand in front of her, his shoulders stiff, his hand instinctively reaching out to shield her. Orion's light-hearted demeanor was gone, replaced by a serious expression that made his face seem older, more hardened.

They were in deep trouble, and they both knew it.

Professor Ember's eyes seemed to darken, to mere slits in the dim light. She wore a black robe, blending into the shadows around her as if it was made of them.

As she stood there, Orion and Elara could feel the air thicken around them.

"Ah, Elara and Orion," she drawled, eyes shone like polished obsidian. "I must say, I didn't expect to find you here."

"Professor Ember," Orion said as he tried to shield the contents of his backpack from view. "We... um, stopped by to see you. We have some questions."

"Oh?" Ember responded, her voice a silk-wrapped blade, each word sharpened with insincere curiosity. Her eyes darted between the two students, studying their expressions with an unsettling intensity. She flicked her wrist and the office door slammed shut and locked. She stood in front of the only way out of the room. "Well, by all means, enlighten me."

Summoning her courage, Elara moved forward. "We've found something disturbing about Professor Mistral's death. We believe you may know more."

Ember's lips curled up into a smirk. "Really now? Why would you think that?"

"Orion spotted you," Elara said, her voice a mixture of fear and defiance, "with the vault key."

"Interesting," Ember said, arching an eyebrow in bemusement. "But it could've been any key. Are you sure it was the one to the vault, children?"

The room seemed to darken at Ember's words, the

shadows deepening around her. For a moment, she said nothing, her eyes narrowed in contemplation. All the while, the black mist that seemed to follow her everywhere continued to billow around her.

"Yes." Orion, emboldened by Elara's courage, took a step forward. "We found the missing artifact from the vault and its key is in your office safe."

Ember's features didn't change, but the office seemed to grow colder, the shadows deepening around her. Her black gaze flicked to the place where Orion had stashed his backpack. "Well, that's... curious."

"Also," Elara said, her voice surprisingly steady despite the cold coming off the professor, "We've learned all about your past and your research into the dark arts."

A moment of tense silence hung in the room. Ember's lips curled into a tight smile. She didn't deny the accusation, nor did she admit it. Instead, she threw her head back and laughed, a sound as chilling as it was mocking.

"Such imaginative minds," Ember said, the corners of her lips twitching into a sardonic smile. "It would be a mistake to jump to conclusions. An artifact in my possession does not make me a thief. As a professor, I need to have access to them, just like all the other teachers," she stated, her voice echoing around the room. "So, before you point fingers, be sure of your facts."

"Maybe," Elara said, her voice growing more courageous by the moment. "But we know you have a history with the Shadows' Grasp."

For a heartbeat, the shadows seemed to deepen around Ember, her lips curling into a smug, devilish smirk. Then, unexpectedly, she laughed again, a sound devoid of warmth. "Very well," she conceded, her voice dripping with pride and arrogance. "It seems I underestimated you both. Yes, I used the Shadows' Grasp to kill Mistral."

For a moment, Elara felt as if the ground beneath her feet disappeared. The words, as they fell from Ember's lips, were unexpected and terrifying. Yes, they had accused her, but hearing her admission of guilt was a chilling reality. The woman standing in front of them, wrapped in shadows and mystery, was a murderer. Elara's heart hammered in her chest like a trapped bird, panic clawing its way up her throat. Elara moved closer to Orion. They were trapped, but at least they were trapped together.

Orion's voice wavered as he asked, "Why... why would you murder Mistrial?"

"Because she was in my way and the do-gooder threatened to expose my secret," Ember replied casually, as if bored. "She was snooping around and uncovered my interest in the Aegis of the Ancients. Mistrial was planning to expose me, which would have ruined everything. Such a vexing situation for me. But I made my choice."

Elara's blood boiled. The professor's confession echoed in her head, the malicious, frosty tone a stark contrast to the warm, nurturing professors like Mistrial. Elara felt an icy dread seep into her bones, knots grew in her stomach. Ember, a professor, a guardian of knowledge, had used her powers to kill.

Elara's mind whirled with the magnitude of the revelation. She wanted to bolt, to escape the room that suddenly felt more like a crypt, oppressive and dark, that had plunged Elara into an unknown world of treachery and danger that she was utterly unprepared for.

"So, you killed her? Just like that?" Elara spat, her hands curling into fists.

"No. It was for power," Ember uttered the word as if it was a mantra. "The lifeblood of our magical realm, child. And that artifact could help me become the most powerful sorceress in the world."

"You have no remorse?" Elara asked, her limbs shaky.

"Such a waste of time." Ember shrugged. "Regret is a luxury I simply can't afford."

"Then your heart must be a black hole," Orion shot back, his voice trembling but resilient. "How can you justify murder in your quest for power?"

Ember merely sneered at Orion's remark. "Whether or not my heart is dark, it has served me well." She stepped further into the room. Behind her a thick slab of shadows blocked the door. "Ah, without a slice of darkness, we are nothing but prey for the shadows that lurk in the depths of our own hearts."

As Ember uttered those words, an eerie movement shrouded the room. The shadows curling around her like grotesque specters rose up, as if they were sentient entities under her command.

Orion's eyes met Elara's. He could see a wave of fear wash over her. The weight of their discovery settled heavily on her chest, making it difficult to draw a breath. They were now burdened with a dangerous secret—the truth behind Mistrial's murder and Ember's monstrous confession.

Ember, however, seemed to revel in their horror. Her eyes, reflecting the dim light, as if to suck all life out of the room. "Speaking of power, I now possess Aegis of the Ancients, and I will be returning it to its rightful place."

"And where's that?" Orion pressed, his voice barely more than a whisper.

"Mythos Isle is home to three distinct schools, Charmcaster Academy, Fantasia School, and Nebulous Institute. I hail from the Nebulous Institute," Ember replied, her words oozing with sinister pleasure. "Unlike this whimsical academy, my alma mater appreciates the potency of dark relics. And that artifact belongs to our academy."

"I don't believe you," Elara said. "You're not just returning a relic to your school, are you?"

"Clever girl." Ember's twisted grin widened at Elara's words. "No, I plan to use Aegis of the Ancients to dissolve the protective enchantments around Mythos Isle first. With it, I will expose our magical world to the mundane humans, causing chaos and confusion. It would give me the perfect opportunity to seize control and reshape this world as I see fit. Keeping the magic a secret from humans is tiresome."

"Y-you're mad!" Orion exclaimed.

"Am I? Or am I simply a visionary?" Ember said, her lips curling into a wicked grin. "No matter, you won't be around to find out. I will create total chaos and then when tire of that I will go down in history as the sorceress that restored peace."

Elara's lips pressed together in a firm line. Her clenched fists trembled slightly.

Elara knew she couldn't let Professor Ember carry out her sinister plan. She exchanged glances with Orion. They had to escape and warn the others. But how?

As if sensing the impending challenge, Ember lifted her hand, her eyes flashing grimly. The room responded to her silent command, shadows condensing around her, swirling and writhing like a gathering storm. Suddenly, the ominous cloud of darkness lashed out, forming a deadly bolt of shadow magic that hurled straight toward them.

Reacting on pure instinct, Orion's hand shot up, an incantation slipping from his lips. From the ancient wooden floorboards beneath them, vines erupted, thick and twisted. They wove together rapidly, forming an organic shield just as the shadow bolt collided with it. The room filled with a low, resonating thud as the attack was repelled, the vines absorbing the impact and keeping them safe, albeit barely.

"Seems we have a stalemate, Professor." Orion gritted his teeth, his heart pounding.

The vines were sturdy, but the intensity of Ember's shadow magic was increasing. The room was getting darker and colder, the shadows extending and contorting, reflecting the escalating hostility.

Elara, though trembling, found her voice. "Orion, the bookshelves!" she gasped.

The towering shelves, previously still and innocuous, were now stirring ominously. Books were flying off, opening to pages inscribed with shadowy glyphs, fluttering like dark-winged birds around Ember.

A sense of dread coursed through them as they realized what was happening. The room was responding to Ember's magic, becoming an extension of her shadowy grasp. Their refuge was transforming into a terrifying labyrinth, the exit morphing into walls, the path to safety turning into a spiraling maze.

The vines shook under another blow of her deadly power.

"She's too powerful!" Orion said, glancing at Elara with a hint of desperation.

Just then, a secret passage unveiled itself behind a massive portrait.

"Run!" he yelled, grabbing his backpack and Elara's hand, pulling her toward the opening. Who knows where it leads, but it has to be safer than where they are at.

They looked at each other and, without a word,

they bolted toward it. They sprinted down the corridor, Ember's rage-filled shouts echoing behind them.

"Stop!" Professor Ember screamed, unleashing another volley of shadow bolts in their direction.

They tried to look behind themselves to duck and dodge the shadow bolts as they ran straight ahead. Elara felt an icy cold cut graze her shoulder, barely missing her. Orion's grip on her hand tightening.

"Hurry, Elara," he urged. "We have to warn the others. We can't let Ember win."

The sound of approaching footsteps sent a shudder down Elara's spine. They were running out of time. Her thoughts were racing almost as fast as their feet. And then it came to her—the one chance they had at escaping Ember's wrath and putting an end to her sinister ambitions.

She tugged him to a stop in the corridor.

"Orion, we need to combine our magic!" Elara shouted.

In perfect sync, Orion and Elara channeled their magic together, their powers melding in a dance as old as time. Orion commanded vines with prickly thorns, as Elara sent a fierce whirlwind across the vines, thicker than any he had ever summoned before. Orion's vines twisted and curled within the tempest, creating a formidable living barrier that pulsed with their combined energy.

Professor Ember's shadow onslaught crashed into the wind-hardened vine barricade with an explosive force, the dark energy ricocheting wildly. The unexpected rebound of her own magic caught Ember off guard, the blowback causing her to stagger back several feet. Her usually composed face twisted momentarily in surprise and frustration, her connection with the shadowy tendrils momentarily distorted.

"Come on!" Orion yelled, his voice raw and desperate. "This is our chance to get to the headmistress!"

Orion and Elara sprinted down the long hallways, racing for Headmistress Nightshade's office.

"Orion, I can't believe she was behind it all," Elara panted between breaths.

"Neither can I," replied Orion. "But we have to tell Nightshade everything—about Ember's sinister plans, about the Shadows' Grasp, the missing artifact."

They rounded a corner, nearly colliding with a group of students who stared at them wide-eyed. But Orion and Elara didn't slow down, their focus singularly set on reaching the headmistress.

Finally, they arrived at the heavy wooden door that

marked Headmistress Nightshade's office. Orion pushed open the door without knocking.

"Headmistress Nightshade." Orion gasped, struggling to catch his breath.

"We have evidence... Professor Ember..." Elara panted, resting her hands on her knees to catch her breath.

"She's behind everything. Mistral's murder, the missing artifact..." Orion sputtered.

"I don't understand, children," Headmistress Nightshade said, her brow furrowing in concern as she took in their frantic state. She stood from her desk and told them, "Catch your breath and start from the beginning."

Elara stepped forward, her voice shaking but resolute. "We found this dossier in the Elysium Archive," she said, grasping Orion's backpack and digging through it until her fingers touched the worn parchment that revealed Ember's past. "It shows that Professor Ember was a researcher of the Shadows' Grasp. Orion, um, found it in your office."

"And," Orion added, his voice steadier now, "we found the vault key that was missing from Professor Mistral's desk. Ember admitted to using the Shadows' Grasp to kill Mistral and steal Aegis of the Ancients for her own sinister purposes." He removed the key and the artifact from the backpack and handed them to the headmistress.

"She tried to kill us," Elara said, her chin quivering. "She used dark magic on us in the school."

Nightshade's eyes seemed to pierce into the items laid out before her, her face a mask of deep concentration. "If what you're saying holds truth, we cannot delay," she said, the gravity in her tone making the room feel warmer. "We appreciate your vigilance, Orion and Elara."

She believed them! Elara thought. She had been worried that the headmistress might dismiss them again. Or worse, be in on it.

A wave of relief washed over Elara. Headmistress Nightshade's belief in them was reassuring, yet Ember still had to be dealt with before she and Orion could feel safe.

Alongside Orion, she retreated to a corner of Nightshade's expansive office. The room was filled with a soft, otherworldly glow, emanating from a lamp fashioned from a crystal that pulsed with ambient magic. Ancient tomes and artifacts of untold powers adorned the shelves, each a testament to Nightshade's extensive knowledge and prowess.

"Stay back," Nightshade instructed, her voice carrying an echo of the celestial power she wielded.

With a stern look etched on her face, she raised her hands, palms upward. As she did so, the room pulsed with an energy so potent it made the hair on the back of Orion's neck stand up. Elara's hair blew in all directions, a force of nature on its own.

Starlight formed in tiny swirling eddies around Nightshade, glimmers of cosmic energy spiraling into existence, conjured from nothingness. With a swift, decisive motion, she pushed the celestial energy outward, toward the center of the room. She created small galaxies right in front of their eyes. Even as far as this academy went, this was pretty far out there as far as magic went.

"Ember," she commanded, her voice echoing with a power that made the room shudder. "Appear before us."

The stars she controlled burst into a dazzling spectacle of light, bending space and time itself. Suddenly, in the whirl of cosmic energy, a figure was wrenched into being. Professor Ember stumbled forward, looking disoriented, her eyes wide with surprise and quickly turning into anger as she found herself facing the headmistress.

"Headmistress Nightshade," Ember acknowledged coolly, her voice betraying no emotion. "I received your summons. What is this about?"

"Please, take a seat, Professor." Nightshade gestured to the chair in front of her desk. There was no kindness in her tone. Ember sat down, her back straight and poised, her floating shadows shrunken to little puffs of fog at her feet. The headmistress continued, "We have reason to believe you're involved in Professor Mistral's death."

"Is that so?" Ember raised an eyebrow, feigning surprise. She cast a dark look at Elara and Orion huddling in the corner. "And what proof do you have of these allegations?"

Nightshade stabbed a finger on top of the dossier on her desk, then flicked her wrist at the key and artifact. "Were these items not found in your possession, Ember? We they not locked away in your office and discovered by two of my students?"

"Plus," Elara said, "we heard your confession when you admitted to killing Professor Mistral using the Shadow Grasp's spell."

Ember's eyes went completely black, but she said nothing.

"Your actions have endangered not only our school but the entire magical world," Nightshade said, her voice heavy with disappointment. "As a result, I have no choice but to strip you of your powers and your position."

Ember scoffed, her voice dripping with sarcasm. "Oh no, what a devastating loss," she replied mockingly. "How will I ever survive without my powers and position? I'm devastated. Boo-hoo."

Headmistress Nightshade's eyes narrowed as she met Ember's sarcasm with a stern gaze. "Your flippant attitude only further demonstrates the depth of your disregard for the responsibility and trust that comes with your powers," she retorted. "This decision is not taken lightly, but it is necessary to protect the safety and integrity of our magical community."

Ember bolted out of her seat, the chair falling over. She ran to the door, but it swung shut before she could escape. Nightshade extended her arm in Ember's direction, her hand opened like a celestial conduit. Elara held her breath, anticipating the forthcoming spectacle of power. Nightshade murmured words that rang with an ancient, melodic rhythm, a spell harnessed from the unfathomable depths of the cosmos.

A dazzling cascade of stellar light burst from her fingertips, the energy shaped by Nightshade's profound will. This spectacle was akin to witnessing a supernova birthed in the confines of an office. The overwhelming brilliance danced across the room, its path unerring as it sought Ember, ensnaring her in its star-born luminosity.

With a gasp, it enveloped Ember in the celestial glow, her body wreathed in its resplendent yet fierce brilliance. The room trembled with the raw power of Nightshade's spell, a silent testament to her control over the untamed cosmos.

As the light subsided, a gasp escaped from Elara. Orion tightened his hold on his friend. Where once Ember's aura pulsed with a dark, relentless force, now it had all but vanished. She stood there, stripped of her shadow magic, her eyes reflecting a harsh truth—she was defeated. The once formidable professor now looked hollow, her vitality erased, her magical essence extinguished. Ember's countenance mirrored her internal plight; pale and forlorn, she was a specter of her former self, bearing the aftermath of Nightshade's celestial retribution.

"Gargoyles will escort you off the premises," Headmistress Nightshade informed her coldly. "Any attempt to return or cause harm to this institution will be met with severe consequences."

Two huge stone gargoyles opened the office door and led Ember away. Elara felt relief course through her.

"Orion, Elara," Nightshade addressed them softly, "you've both shown immense bravery and resourcefulness. Thank you for protecting our world."

CHAPTER SEVENTEEN

W eeks flew by in a blur. The looming
Otherworld Triad Tournament added a
frenetic edge to life at Charmcaster Academy. Orion's days were filled with honing his
plant magic, attending classes, and studying. While
trying to carve out a little time to spend with Ivy and
the rest of the group. The academy, once haunted by
the shadow of Professor Ember's treachery, now
buzzed with eager students trading tales of past tourna-
ments. And yet, the chilling memory of Professor
Ember's betrayal was like a dull throb in the back of his
mind, a reminder that the world of magic was more
complex and scarier than he had ever imagined.

Today, Orion stood at the edge of the training

grounds, his eyes scanning the vast expanse before him. His heart pounded with excitement as an elemental surge of energy coursed through him. The Otherworld Triad Tournament was approaching, and there was no time to waste. He glanced over at Elara, who was adjusting her pale hair into a ponytail. She leaned forward, her posture becoming more upright. The fire in her gaze burned brighter, reflecting the unwavering resolve within her.

Beside them, Zara and Flint were stretching their muscles, readying themselves for the intense training session ahead. In front of them stood Professor Frostwood, who was assisting the head trainer, Professor Swiftwater.

"All right, students," Professor Swiftwater said, his booming voice cutting through the chilly air like a dull blade. "You know why we're here, Charmcasters, and it's preparing you for the tournament."

Winning would bring great honor to Charmcaster Academy, and the thought only fueled Orion's goals to succeed. After everything, his father's words still gave him the encouragement he needed. "*You're tougher than you think.*"

"Listen carefully and follow our instructions," added Professor Frostwood, her cool demeanor contrasting sharply with her colleague's enthusiasm.

"We'll be pushing you harder than ever before, so stay focused and give it your all."

The students stood in a line at the edge of the training grounds, their eyes wide with raw determination. The landscape was alive with fall's vibrant colors; the grassy hills were sprinkled with wildflowers of all colors, the trees rustled in the wind, and the rocky plateaus glistened in the sun's golden light.

As Orion took it all in, the winds carrying the scent of blossoming flowers and fresh-cut grass through his clothes, he felt a rush of strength and power. He didn't have to search for it, it was in him, just under the surface.

Orion felt a surge of magic pulse through him, animating the plants surrounding him. Vibrant leaves rustled, reaching out to brush against him as if in greeting. The natural world responded to Orion's presence, acknowledging his connection to the mystical forces that flowed through him.

"Begin with a warmup lap around the perimeter," instructed Professor Swiftwater.

The four friends took off at a brisk pace, their breaths coming out in foggy puffs as they navigated the uneven terrain.

Orion felt his legs burn as he leaped over fallen logs and ducked under low-hanging branches, the crisp air filling his lungs. He could hear Elara's steady breaths beside him, as well as Zara's occasional grunt of effort, and Flint's heavy footfalls were behind that. The challenges of the training grounds were both exhilarating and exhausting, but Orion knew they were designed to push the students to their limits and beyond.

As they rounded a steep hill, Orion's eyes widened in awe as a magical obstacle course came into view. It was a whimsical assortment of floating wooden planks, defying gravity. Narrow beams balanced gracefully on tall poles, and swinging ropes, like jungle vines, dangled from towering treetops. The air was thick with excitement and sweat.

"All right!" called out Professor Frostwood, blowing a whistle. "Time to put your skills to the test! Each of you will navigate the course using your unique abilities."

Orion exchanged a glance with Elara, Flint, and Zara before they each set off on their individual paths.

As he climbed the first shaky platform, Orion thought about the upcoming tournament. Winning wouldn't just bring honor to Charmcaster Academy; it would also prove to himself and everyone else that he had what it took to be a powerful Charmcaster. With that thought spurring him on, Orion pushed himself harder than ever before.

Zara stepped forward first, her eyes narrowed in concentration. She raised her hands, fingers splayed, and a crackling fireball materialized in the air above them. With a fluid motion, she propelled it toward one of the suspended planks. The wood ignited instantly, turning into ash within seconds.

"Excellent control, Zara," commended Professor Frostwood. Beside the teacher, a pen, guided by an invisible hand, etched an account of Zara's performance onto a floating parchment. Suspended in mid-air by an unseen magical force, the document fluttered lightly with each stroke, the ink shimmering with faint, mystic radiance as it settled onto the page. How else could a professor take notes?

Flint approached the trembling beam next, his expression firm. He slammed his fist against the ground, causing the earth beneath him to rise and envelop the narrow structure. The formerly unsteady beam was now encased in solid rock, providing Flint with solid footing as he crossed.

"Good improvisation, Flint," praised Professor Swiftwater. "Orion! You're up next."

Orion's pulse thundered in his ears, his heart dancing to the rhythm of eager anticipation. He locked onto the nearest tree, letting his magic answer his silent call. It rose within him, a simmering warmth that spread from his heart, down his veins, and all the way to the tips of his fingers.

With a flick of his wrist, a vibrant vine erupted from the tree's rough bark, snaking through the air to wrap around Orion's waist. He gave a delighted gasp as it hoisted him up, his feet leaving the ground in a swift, seamless motion.

As he swung from one tree to the next, guided by the sentient plants he'd come to think of as friends, pride welled up within him. Each successful swing was a testament to his growing mastery over his unique gift, a magical bond between him and the plant kingdom that he wouldn't trade for anything.

He landed softly back on the ground and smiled.

"Your precision has improved immensely, Orion!" Professor Frostwood said, her eyes gleaming with encouragement.

Elara was the last to step forward. Her eyes gleamed with unyielding focus. With an elegant twirl, she unleashed her magic, her movements fluid and precise, commanding the attention of all who watched. A gust of wind answered her summons, whipping around her like a cyclone in miniature. The wind swept her upwards, cradling her as though she weighed no more than a leaf, and propelled her from platform to platform. She moved with an uncanny grace that seemed to defy gravity itself, each leap executed with the precision of a hunting falcon.

The surrounding wind danced to her tune, spiraling and whirling like a miniature cyclone, a clear testament to her command over her wind magic.

Orion stared at his best friend, captivated by her strength and grace, as she wielded her magic with the ease of a true wind charmer.

"Superb finesse, Elara," Professor Swiftwater remarked, nodding approvingly.

"Everyone, gather 'round!" Professor Frostwood shouted. "Now that we've seen what you can do individually, let's see how well you can combine your powers to show us how you handle teamwork. Remember, collaboration and communication are essential." He pointed up at a tangle of trees where an obstacle course was suspended in air.

Again, Zara and Flint went first. They stood side by side, their faces set with fierce determination. With a swift, assertive gesture, Flint raised his arms, pulling from the depths of his earth magic. The air rippled as chunks of rock pulled from the ground, ascending into the sky to form a rocky bridge through the treacherous obstacle course. Simultaneously, Zara flamed up, her fire magic wrapping around her like a radiant aura. With a whoosh, she transformed into a vibrant firebird, illuminating the sky. As Flint maneuvered the floating rocky path, Zara darted around him, her flames incinerating obstacles and creating a blazing shield. Together, they conquered the course, a seamless dance of fire and earth high above the ground.

When they landed on the ground, they each took a bow. Orion and Elara clapped and cheered.

"Outstanding work, Zara and Flint!" Professor Swiftwater exclaimed, clapping his hands together in excitement. "That was a brilliant display of synergy. Your earth and fire magic complement each other perfectly. Your ability to anticipate each other's movements and act in unison turned a challenging obstacle course into a mere child's play," Professor Frostwood said. "Keep harnessing this teamwork, and there will be no obstacle you can't overcome. Well done!"

"Your turn, Orion and Elara," Swiftwater said. Motioning for them to step up.

Orion exchanged an excited glance with Elara as they stepped forward. Orion knew that using their elemental abilities together would form a formidable duo.

"Ready?" he asked her, his voice steady and sure.

"Always," she replied with a confident smile.

Brimming with unfaltering focus, Orion honed his concentration on his flora skills. The already familiar sensation of heat coursed through his veins, a vibrant reminder of the power he commanded. With a swift, sweeping gesture, a robust kudzu vine sprang forth from his outstretched hand, its tendrils binding securely around Elara's wrist like a lifeline.

No sooner had the vine clasped onto Elara than she cast herself into the open air. A gust of wind, manipulated by her influence, swirled around her in an airy cocoon. The wind, at her command, whipped around them, capturing not only Elara but also the vine within its uplifting spiral.

The gusty vortex gave momentum to the vine, its strength buoyed by the wind's force. With the vine and wind working in unison, Orion found himself able to swing deftly alongside Elara. Their journey through the aerial course unfolded like an intricate dance, a testament to their harmonized control over their unique elemental gifts. Their close friendship for sure impacted the way their magic blended together.

"Amazing synchronization!" Professor Swiftwater exclaimed.

Orion's vines, like agile serpents, slithered and coiled in response to Elara's winds, forming complex nets and catapults. Elara's wind gusts swirled and danced, reacting to Orion's green tendrils, lifting and propelling them with impressive precision.

Their classmates watched, cheering, and clapping. As the last obstacle was cleared, Orion and Elara landed gracefully on the ground, panting slightly but grinning from ear to ear.

"Absolutely phenomenal," Professor Frostwood declared, her eyes shining with pride. "Outstanding control for first year Charmcasters, bravo."

Professor Swiftwater smiled. "Your teamwork is truly commendable. Keep up the good work, and you'll be unstoppable in the tournament."

Orion beamed at the praise and his confidence grew. Elara threw up a high-five that he almost missed.

Professor Frostwood gave all the students a warm smile. "Now that we've seen what each of you is capable of, let's discuss the upcoming tournament in more detail." She waved her hand, and an intricate model of the arena rose from the ground, complete with miniature stands and varied terrains. "Welcome to the Otherworld Triad Tournament," she said, her icy stare sweeping over the group of students. "The main event will consist of several trials, each designed to test your magical skills. The next one will showcase team-work and adaptability. You will face formidable opponents from the Fantasia School of Sea and Shifters, a renowned academy known for its powerful animal and sea shifting students."

Flint's brow furrowed. "We'll be facing water and shape-shifting magicians?"

"That is correct." Professor Frostwood nodded gravely. "Their abilities are not to be underestimated. They have trained hard and will undoubtedly prove challenging adversaries. But I have faith in each of you. Your talents have grown immensely, and if you continue to work together as you have today, I believe we can emerge victorious."

Orion caught Elara's gaze, her eyes sparking with that familiar steel-like resolve. He could practically feel the heavy pressure of what they were up against, like a solid wall to walk through. But there was something else too, an undercurrent of confidence. Their shared experiences had knit a bond between them that no vine could break. Even the gnarliest challenges seemed less intimidating when they stood together as a team.

"Professor, what happens if we win?" Zara asked.

"Victory would bring honor to Charmcaster Academy, of course," Professor Frostwood replied, a hint of a smile crossing her lips. "But more importantly, it would grant us use of Aegis of the Ancients, an artifact of immense power and significance."

Orion scanned the faces of his friends, catching the eyes of his classmates, their expressions a blend of pumped-up excitement and gnawing nerves. He understood they were all feeling the pressure. But there was this thrilling, almost intoxicating pull of this victory—a shining trophy just barely within reach.

"Rest assured," Professor Swiftwater said, "we will do everything in our power to prepare you for this tournament. I believe that each of you has the potential to rise to the occasion."

"Sea and Shifters ain't got nothing on us!" Flint declared, his voice full of male bravado.

"Absolutely!" Orion chimed in, his eyes shining with a new determination. He instinctively balled his hands into fists. "We're all in, ready to face any challenge head on."

"As long as we stick together, nothing can stop us. So yeah, we've got this," Elara added, her pale cheeks flushed red from exertion.

Professor Swiftwater cleared his throat, his usually warm eyes holding a serious glint. "Listen carefully, students," he began, a sober edge to his voice. "This tournament will push your magical abilities and test your courage like nothing before. It is a daunting challenge filled with unexpected obstacles and perilous tasks..."

Smiles fell from their faces, and Orion felt his shoulders slump. Elara grew quiet and serious again.

Swiftwater paused, ensuring he had their undivided attention. "The dangers you'll face will be very real. You must be prepared for anything and everything. Success in this tournament requires not just raw power, but strategy, teamwork, and a profound respect for the potential consequences. This is not just a game. Your safety is my paramount concern, so please, take this warning to heart."

Professor Frostwood clapped her hands, drawing the attention of the group. "Allow me to tell you more about Aegis of the Ancients. The artifact dates back to the time of the first Charmcaster civilization and is said to possess abilities beyond our comprehension." She paced before them, her eyes full of seriousness. "The relic is believed to grant the wielder immense magical power, and to provide protection against dark forces, making it an invaluable asset in our ongoing fight against evil."

"Wow," breathed Elara, her eyes wide with wonder. "No pressure."

Orion shared her fascination—and concern. His mind reeling from the potential power of the ancient artifact.

Images of Professor Ember, with her wicked smile, flashed through his mind. He remembered the way she had coveted Aegis of the Ancients, hungering for its power to spread chaos and destruction. It was a sobering reminder of how close they had come to catastrophe. He and Elara had exposed her dark plot before she could wield Aegis of the Ancients' immense power, but the memory of her malicious intent was a scar that refused to fade. He was still having nightmares about Professor Mistral and lately he's had a hard time falling asleep in his dark dorm room thinking the shadows were out to get him.

"Then we must win the tournament," Flint declared, his voice unwavering. "We cannot let such power slip away."

"No way are we losing," Zara said. "We got this, Professor."

Orion felt a surge of excitement course through him. He envisioned himself winning the tournament. His thoughts turned to his family, who would undoubtedly be proud of him if he played a part in securing such a powerful artifact for Charmcaster Academy. "*You're going to do amazing things.*"

"I like your grit," Professor Frostwood said. "But Fantasia School will be a formidable opponent. You must train harder than ever before and trust in your abilities whole heartedly."

Professor Swiftwater added, "We will guide you and help you hone your skills. We believe in each one of you."

"Thank you, professors," Elara said.

Orion felt a sense of camaraderie and purpose as he looked around at his classmates, his friends. They were in this together, and they would face the upcoming tournament as one.

As Orion watched the sun slide under the horizon, it painted long, stretching shadows across the training grounds. Professor Swiftwater and Frostwood called out their final instructions for the day, their voices carried off by the crisp wind that hinted at the impending winter. His eyes followed the last rays of sunlight as they disappeared, a light jacket of twilight replacing the warmth of day, carrying a hint of the season's turn in the earthy scent of fallen leaves.

"You are strong, capable, Charmcasters. Don't ever forget that." Professor Swiftwater added, his voice warm and reassuring.

With a final nod, the professors dismissed the students, who began filing out of the training grounds.

Watching as his friends drifted away, Orion felt the magnitude of the approaching tournament thump heavily in his chest. The upcoming days, he knew, were about to be chock-full of relentless training and high-strung nerves. But as daunting as the tournament was, he could also sense an electric pulse of unity threading through everyone. He glanced at Elara, her determined face mirroring his own. Together with their peers, they were in this fight to the finish, set on giving everything they had to keep the ancient relic right where it belonged—at Charmcaster Academy.

Ivy approached them as they entered the courtyard.

"Hey guys! Have you heard any more about Ember?" Ivy asked hesitantly, her green eyes wide with curiosity. "I mean, where did go after she was stripped of her magic and booted off campus?"

"Professor Nightshade hasn't shared much about it," Orion admitted, his stomach churning at the thought of the recent events. "I'm just glad she was caught."

"Me too and it just motivates me even more to win," Elara said, her long hair whipping around her face as a breeze picked up.

"Right," Ivy agreed. "This tournament is about protecting our world and the academy."

Orion fell silent, mulling over their words and the immense responsibility that now rested on their shoulders.

When they neared the dormitories, he knew one thing for certain: they couldn't afford to lose. The stakes were higher than ever before, and it was up to them to ensure the safety of Aegis of the Ancients.

"Let's get some rest," Elara said softly, sensing the heavy thoughts weighing on everyone's minds. "Tomorrow, we'll train harder than ever."

As they reached the hallway that branched off to the dorms, they were met by a smiling Headmistress Nightshade. She beckoned them to come over, her dark-purple robes billowing around her.

"Orion, Elara, I wanted to commend you both for your exceptional progress and dedication to our academy," she said warmly. "Your courage and loyalty to this school has not gone unnoticed. In recognition of your commitment, we'll be presenting each of you with an enchanted pendant. It's designed to amplify your magic during the tournament, a token of our appreciation."

"Wow! Thanks," Orion replied.

"Thank you, Headmistress Nightshade," Elara whispered, her eyes shining with gratitude.

"Make us proud, you two," Headmistress Nightshade said, her voice firm but encouraging. She whirled around and dashed off.

He couldn't let anyone down. Orion knew—they all did—there was no turning back now. They were in this together, prepared to tackle whatever the tournament might throw at them, with one common goal: victory.

CHAPTER EIGHTEEN

Elara's pulse spiked as she stood in front of the full-length mirror, her hands trembling ever so slightly. Today was the day she had been training for—the Otherworld Triad Tournament. Her hands trembled and her heart raced. A combination of apprehension and eagerness rushed through her body, fueling her unwavering determination to prove herself worthy of winning this competition. She couldn't let her friends down, especially Orion, who had worked just as hard as her to prepare. Elara closed her eyes, took a deep breath, and slowly exhaled, trying to steady her nerves.

"Are you ready?" Aria, her roommate, asked from behind her.

Elara opened her eyes and nodded. "As ready as I'll ever be."

Aria gave her arm a reassuring squeeze. "I know you'll do great."

"Thanks," Elara replied, offering a small smile before turning her attention back to her reflection.

She wore the Charmcaster Academy uniform—a white blouse with puffed sleeves tucked into a black skirt, adorned with delicate purple embroidery along the collar. A fitted black waistcoat with gleaming buttons completed the ensemble, and a silver pendant in the shape of a tornado hung around her neck, symbolizing her affinity for wind magic.

Elara pulled her hair back into a tight ponytail, not a single strand out of place. A subtle touch of purple eyeshadow framed her eyes, matching the school colors.

"Wow," Aria remarked, her voice laced with pride. "You look every bit the fierce competitor."

"Thanks," Elara said again, finally pulling herself away from the mirror. "I just hope I can live up to everyone's expectations."

"Hey," Aria said, placing a hand on Elara's shoulder. "You've trained hard for this. You're going to be amazing."

Elara took another deep breath and nodded, her

eyes meeting Aria's steady gaze. "You're right. I can do this."

Elara straightened her posture and squared her shoulders and left the room. She was ready to represent Charmcaster Academy with pride, and to fight for victory in the Otherworld Triad Tournament.

A few minutes later, Elara's heart raced as she stood with Orion in the castle's foyer, facing the courtyard. They waited for the moment that would transport them to the Arcane Arena. The Otherworld Triad Tournament was by far the most prestigious magical competition in existence, fought between elite schools of the mystical arts.

"Orion," Elara whispered, leaning in closer to her friend. Her excitement shimmered in her eyes. "I can't believe we're really doing this. The Otherworld Triad Tournament is a massive deal. I never thought flying unicorns would take me to school and now this? Crazy."

He fidgeted with his glasses, his nervousness palpable. "I know, it's intense. But hey, we've put in the hours, the sweat, and the magic. We'll give it our all and make Charmcaster Academy shine."

Elara's lips curled into a confident grin as she inhaled deeply, her breath steadying her racing heart. A surge of energy pulsed through her veins, propelling her courage with unwavering certainty. "You're right. Let's show them what we're made of!"

Professor Swiftwater, his turquoise robes billowing like an ocean current, approached the pair. "Listen closely," he began, his voice laden with wisdom and caution. "The Otherworld Triad Tournament, started by the founding headmasters centuries ago, is a time-honored tradition. While safety is paramount, the nature of magic and the intense competition can present risks. Your training, knowledge, and unity will be crucial. Follow instructions, support one another, and represent our academy with honor and resilience." His smile filled the chamber, his voice echoing.

"Yes, Professor," Orion answered, cracking his knuckles.

"Very well." Professor Swiftwater drew a circle in the air with his hand, murmuring incantations under his breath. Silvery-blue light emanated from his fingers, forming a shimmering portal before them. "Step through, and you will find yourself at the Arcane Arena."

Elara glanced at Orion, who gave her a reassuring smile. She took a deep breath, gathering her courage to step through the portal. A rush of icy air enveloped her, causing her to shiver involuntarily. The sensation of weightlessness made her stomach lurch, and just as quickly as it had started, Elara stood on solid ground. Orion appeared beside her and grinned.

They stood in a waiting area of the arena draped with long, flowing banners of vivid colors, depicting powerful warriors and mythical creatures. They composed the walls of large stones held together by shimmering strands of magic, and they made the floor out of smooth, polished marble. The room had the faint smell of scorched earth mixed with the sweet aroma of freshly cut grass.

From outside the arena, they could hear the faint roar of excited crowds, reverberating through the halls and giving a sense of urgency and excitement.

"Welcome to the Arcane Arena!" a disembodied voice boomed overhead.

"This is awesome," Orion said as he stepped closer to an opening that led to the arena and he peered out.

Arcane Arena was a marvel of magical architecture, its stone walls glimmering with enchantments and pulsating with power. In the center lay the battleground, where they would soon test their abilities against the other schools.

"Focus, you two," Professor Swiftwater's voice came from behind them. "Remember your training and trust in each other. You've got this."

"Thanks, Professor," Elara replied, trying to calm her nerves. She glanced at Orion, who nodded firmly.

"Let's do this," he said, his voice full of resolve.

"All ears on me, magical folks!" the announcer's voice reverberated across the Arcane Arena, a sonic boom that snagged every eye and ear. "Steel your nerves and hold your breath for the ultimate magical clash! Today, we have the dynamic prodigies of Charm-caster Academy going head-to-head with the formidable powerhouses of the Fantasia School of Sea and Shifters! Welcome, one and all, to the Otherworld Triad Tournament, where magic will collide, and legends will be born!"

As Elara and Orion waited in the underground alcove adjacent to the arena, Zara and Flint joined them.

Elara was glad she didn't have to battle either of them. Zara, a fierce African American girl with flaw-less copper colored skin and red-streaked black hair, exuded a haughty personality that matched her mastery of fire magic. Though she was a sweet friend, the gang agreed that you definitely wanted to stay on her good side. Flint, a muscular young man with a square face and thick neck, possessed the formidable ability to manipulate soil, stone, and minerals, making him a formidable opponent. If he ever practiced in dark magic, he could literally split the Earth in half.

"Listen up, everyone," Orion said. "We're in this together. Trust and support each other, and we'll come out on top!"

Elara's ponytail swished behind her as she nodded. "Exactly! Charmcaster Academy is all about teamwork. Let's show the other schools what we're made of!"

Zara's fiery spirit burned brightly as she nodded in agreement. "You bet!"

Flint's nonchalant demeanor didn't hide his confidence. "Yeah, no worries. I've got this." Elara assumed he had to be a ball of nerves too, but he hid it well.

"First up," announced the disembodied MC once more, "we have Zara and Flint from Charmcaster Academy competing in individual challenges against their opponents from the Fantasia School!"

Flint and Zara walked out of the waiting area and onto the main floor of the arena.

Zara flexed her fingers, crimson sparks igniting at her fingertips. Her opponent, a tall girl with long, flowing aquamarine hair, smirked confidently as torrents of water swirled around her.

"May the best Charmcaster win," Zara challenged, her voice full of bravado.

"You're going down, Charmcaster," the girl from

Fantasia School replied coolly, her eyes locked on Zara's.

Flint stood opposite a boy with shaggy, sea-green hair, who appeared to be shifting between a human and a tiger, his body sprouting some fur and fangs. Flint clenched his fists, causing the ground beneath him to tremble slightly.

"Let's do this," Flint growled, his voice tinged with a steely resolve. His jaw clenched, muscles tense, as he prepared himself for battle.

"Bring it on," the shifter responded, a wicked grin spreading across his face.

As the challenges began, Orion and Elara watched intently, their hearts pounding in unison.

"Let the first challenge begin!" boomed the announcer's voice, echoing across the Arcane Arena. "The rules of the battle are simple. Each person can only rely on their magical abilities, and the student to subdue or incapacitate their opponents will be declared the winner."

No sooner had the words left his mouth than the arena transformed. A mighty torrent of water appeared around the competitors, interspersed with jagged rock formations.

"Go!" shouted Professor Swiftwater from the sideline, his booming voice easily reaching Zara and Flint amid the chaos.

"Flint, provide me with cover!" Zara yelled, her eyes locked on the watery foe before her.

Elara knew Zara needed to neutralize the water-wielder quickly to stand a chance in this battle.

"Got it!" Flint replied, slamming his fists into the ground.

Earth and rock rose around Zara, shielding her from the powerful waves sent crashing toward them by the Fantasia School competitor.

Within her makeshift fortress, Zara focused on her amazing fire magic, summoning a searing blaze in her palms. With a cry, she unleashed the inferno, watching as it roared toward the wall of water. Steam billowed as fire met water, creating a cloud of scalding mist that obscured the battlefield. Zara grinned, satisfied with her handiwork.

"Your turn, Flint!" she called out, as if trusting that her teammate would use the distraction to his advantage.

Meanwhile, the shifter boy lunged at Flint, transforming into a fierce tiger in midair, its powerful claws aiming for his throat. Flint barely managed to dodge the attack, using his earth manipulation to create a barrier between himself and the ferocious beast.

"Nice try," Flint taunted, his voice dripping with sarcasm. "But you'll have to do better than that!"

"Careful what you wish for!" the shifter snarled, clawing through the gaps in Flint's defenses.

"Watch out!" Zara shouted, alarmed by the sudden change in tactics.

Flint's eyes widened as he realized the danger he was in, then narrowed. "Got it!" he replied, using his magic to encase the tiger in solid rock before it could strike.

With their opponents now trapped, Zara and Flint exchanged victorious grins as they headed back to the waiting area.

"Charmcaster Academy is the winner of this round!" said the announcer, prompting a wave of applause from the stands.

As the cheers died down, Elara and Orion exchanged nervous glances. It was finally their turn to face their own challenge.

"You're up, plant whisperer," Flint said, clapping Orion on the back.

Zara and Flint took seats on a stone bench. Professor Swiftwater handed them both a bottled water.

The arena shifted once more, this time revealing an enormous tree at its center, its branches reaching high into the sky. Elara looked out over the coliseum and sucked in a breath. Bile rose up in her throat, but she kept it down.

From the Charmcaster Academy side of the arena, an uproarious cheer tore through the stands. Students and professors alike sprang to their feet, their cloaks billowing. Their cheers were fierce, their pride for their school echoing across the arena as they waved banners embroidered with the silver charms that signified Charmcaster Academy.

On the opposite side, the Fantasia School's section was a vibrant spectacle in its own right. With every surge of magic from their champions, the shapeshifters transformed in excitement—feathers ruffled, scales shimmered, and fur bristled. The roar of the beasts and the melodious songs of the mermaids formed a hypnotizing chorus, their boos and cheers ebbing and flowing on the breeze.

"Ladies and gentlemen, hold on to your broomsticks," the announcer said. "The Fantasia School has selected their best shifters for this next challenge..."

Elara stopped listening as two tall, confident students strolled into the arena. She stood at the edge of the opening, her eyes fixated on the intense spectacle unfolding before her. The two students from the rival school, their faces etched with determination, engaged in a fierce challenge. The air crackled with anticipation as they showcased their formidable skills, seamlessly executing intricate spells and maneuvers.

When they'd finished, the crowd erupted in applause. The students smugly left the arena and into their own alcove across the stadium.

"Prepare for a spectacle!" the announcer's voice thundered across the arena. "Next on the battlefield are Orion Evergreen and Elara Silverwind. Their challenge? A test of wits and magic as they must unearth a magical orb hidden in a maze of foliage! Watch as they weave together their mighty wind and plant manipulation skills in this thrilling task. Brace yourselves for a mesmerizing show of Charmcasting!"

"Ready?" Elara asked, her heart thudding against her chest.

"Yes," Orion replied, his gaze unwavering and his expression resolute. His brows furrowed with a focused intensity.

Elara's heart thudded in her chest as she and Orion stepped into the arena.

The towering tree cast its colossal presence upon them, its branches extending like a labyrinth of shadows and leaves. Elara could sense the power of the wind, a gentle caress that shifted and swirled around her, whispering words of encouragement. It wrapped around her like a supportive embrace, urging her to push forward and conquer the challenges that lay ahead. The soft rustle of the leaves seemed to carry messages of resilience and strength.

"Let's split up," Orion suggested. "I'll control the plants to create a path for you while you use your wind magic to scout for the orb."

"Sounds good," Elara agreed, nodding at her friend.

Elara watched as Orion's concentration sharpened as he directed his magic toward the tree. His hands danced through the air, tracing intricate patterns with purpose. Vines and branches responded to his command, coiling and intertwining to form a staircase that spiraled around the towering trunk.

Elara sensed the intensity radiating from him, a mix of strain and an unyielding spark evident in his furrowed brow and the fiery resolve that blazed in his eyes.

"Go!" he urged, giving her a reassuring smile.

Elara's nod was resolute as she catapulted herself onto the first branch, her wind magic surging with raw energy, propelling her upward with exhilarating speed. Each leap she took unleashed powerful gusts of wind, causing the leaves to dance and whirl up a frenzy around her. She scoured the surroundings, her senses heightened and razor-focused amidst the swirling chaos of the foliage. The air crackled with her power as she searched for any glimmer of the elusive magical orb, her senses sharp and focused.

"Anything?" Orion called from below, sweat beading on his brow as he maintained the spell.

"Nothing yet!" Elara replied, gritting her teeth.

The wind wrapped around her, swirling with an electric energy that made the leaves dance and whispered secrets in her ear. Amid the swirling chaos, a teasing glimmer of light appeared, playing tricks on her senses. Her heart raced as a burst of vivid, shimmering color grabbed her attention, briefly illuminating the shadowy surroundings. It was like stumbling upon a hidden treasure, a radiant gem tucked within the leafy curtain, enticing her to chase after its mysterious allure.

"Orion! I found it!" she exclaimed, pointing toward a well-concealed hollow in the tree.

"Great! Hold on!" Orion said, concentrating on the tree once more.

The branches and vines around Elara writhed and twisted, forming a narrow pathway that led to the coveted orb. She extended her trembling hand, ready to seize the prize.

But just as her fingertips grazed its surface, a ferocious gust of wind howled from the opposite direction, threatening to throw her off balance. Her heart pounded in her chest as she fought to regain her footing, her grip on the branch slipping perilously. Every instinct screamed at her to hold on, to conquer the tempest and claim her victory.

"Elara!" Orion cried out in alarm. "Be careful!"

"Thanks for the warning," Elara muttered, her focus sharpening as she regained her balance.

The realization hit her like a thunderclap—amidst the howling wind, she recognized the signs of a calculated counter-spell, a deliberate attempt to protect the precious orb. A surge of adrenaline coursed through her, igniting an unyielding fire within. She braced herself against the opposing forces, channeling her own magic to push back and break through the resistance.

"Orion! I need your help!" she shouted, reaching out her hand toward him. "We got to do this together!"

Without a moment's hesitation, Orion merged his magic with Elara's, channeling his power into the surrounding plants. Tendrils of vibrant green sprouted and entwined around her, providing a solid anchor against the relentless wind. Elara's gaze hardened as she summoned every ounce of her wind magic, gathering it into a swirling vortex that grew in strength and ferocity.

With a resounding roar, her tempestuous gusts clashed and overpowered the opposing forces, creating a fierce battleground within the canopy of the trees.

"*Now!*" she yelled, and together, they reached for the orb.

Their fingers brushed against the smooth surface, and in that instant, the spectators sitting in the arena fell silent.

"Charmcaster Academy wins!" the announcer's voice boomed, echoing throughout the coliseum.

The Charmcaster Academy crowd erupted in a cheer as their champions executed another dazzling display of magic. A sea of fluttering cloaks in every hue imaginable painted a vibrant tapestry of support. The professors' normally composed faces lit with the fervor of the tournament, while the students echoed their support by casting harmless sparks and shimmering illusions that danced in the air.

"We did it!" Elara beamed at Orion beside her.

"Congratulations!" Professor Swiftwater yelled from the sidelines, clapping his hands together with a thunderous crash.

CHAPTER NINETEEN

"Hold on to your magic wands, folks!" the announcer's voice roared across the stadium, crackling with magical energy that roused every spectator. "Brace yourselves for the thunderous thrill of round two in the heart-stopping, pulse-pounding spectacle that is the Otherworld Triad Tournament!"

Orion's heart raced as the announcer's voice reverberated throughout the stadium, signaling the commencement of round two in the Otherworld Triad Tournament. Sweat beaded on h Orion's forehead, and his hands trembled with a mixture of fear and excitement. The tension was palpable, a living thing that twisted around him like tangling weeds, feeding on the anticipation and competitive spirit. He clenched his fists, feeling the familiar weight of responsibility settling on his shoulders.

The crowd erupted into cheers and applause as students from various schools jumped to their feet, waving banners and shouting encouragement for their teams.

Spectators from Charmcaster Academy, clad in their distinctive black, purple, and white uniforms, rumbled with enthusiasm, their faces painted with symbols of power and unity. Among them, Head-mistress Nightshade leaned forward, her intense gaze never leaving the battlefield.

To Orion's left, the Fantasia School attendees were equally boisterous. Clad in robes of vibrant greens and gold, they chanted their school's name in unison, creating a pulsating rhythm that reverberated throughout the stadium. Their faces bore wicked grins, reflecting an unsettling confidence.

Orion shivered, wondering what opponents awaited his friends in this terrifying second round.

Amidst the deafening clamor, Orion's heart swelled with pride for his school and teammates. But deep down, even though he had won the last challenge, a flicker of doubt ignited, whispering of potential fail-ure. He swallowed hard, steeling himself against the encroaching anxiety, determined to prove his worth and silence the nagging voice of insecurity once and for all.

"Stay in the zone, Orion," he murmured to himself, his breath fogging up his black-framed glasses. "I've come a long way since I first stepped foot in this place. I've grown stronger, more confident. I can handle whatever comes my way."

"Orion?" Elara said, touching his arm. "You okay?"

"Yep," he said. "Bring it on!"

She laughed. "Yeah! Those shifters are going down."

With that, Orion took a deep breath and braced himself for the battle that was about to begin. The cheering of the crowd filled his ears, drowning out all other thoughts as he concentrated on proving that Charmcaster Academy was not to be underestimated.

In the waiting area beside him, Elara's chest rose and fell rapidly, her eyes darting around as she muttered a series of incantations under her breath, preparing herself for the battlefield. Her blonde ponytail swayed as she practiced her wind magic, the air around her rippling with power.

Flint cracked his knuckles, a gritty look etched on his square face. Muscles bulging beneath his clothes, he pounded one fist into the palm of his other hand, ready to wield his earth manipulation abilities.

Zara stood tall and resolute, dark eyes narrowed, focused. The fire within her burned bright, her body emanating a tangible heat.

"Prepare yourselves," the announcer's voice erupted, causing the arena to tremble with anticipation. "Stepping into the spotlight first, Charmcaster Academy presents Flint Rockwell, the wizard who makes the very earth dance, and Zara Pyre, a hothead who lights up the arena with her fiery magic!"

The crowd erupted, cheering their favorites.

"But let's not forget their competition!" The announcer's voice boomed over the din, the crowd falling into a hush. "Here comes Naga Blackwood, the snake-shifter who slithers past every challenge, and Drego Sharpfang, the shark-shifter whose power matches the ferocity of the great white himself!"

Flint and Zara stepped onto the battlefield. As they moved toward the center, their opponents from Fantasia School emerged from the shadows.

The opponent, Naga Blackwood, was a girl with striking, angular features that gave her an otherworldly allure. Silvery-blue scales shimmered across her arms, neck, and face, reflecting the light with an eerie glow. Every motion she made flowed like a snake, her body moving with serpentine grace.

Drego Sharpfang, a formidable opponent, stood tall and confident before Flint. His presence was as striking as the ocean's depths, with sharp features that mirrored the strength and resilience of a shark. As he moved, there was a hint of power in his every step, reminiscent of a predator. Drego's fingers elongated into sharp and sleek claws, mirroring the deadly grace of a shark's fin slicing through the water.

"Let the battle begin!" shouted the announcer, and the crowd's roar reached a crescendo.

Orion and Elara watched them face off their opponents on the battlefield. Amidst the chaos of the battle, Orion's heart pounded with adrenaline as he watched the clash between Flint and the shark shifter unfold. Part of him was glad he wasn't in this battle. The arena trembled with the force of their powers colliding, water and earth meeting in a cataclysmic clash. Flint's muscles flexed as he summoned towering walls of stone from the ground, countering the relentless onslaught of the shark shifter's watery attacks. The earth shook beneath their feet, sending shockwaves through the air, while he filled the arena with the echoing roar of crashing waves and the sharp snap of powerful jaws.

"Flint! Behind you!" Zara shouted, her eyes wide as

Drego whirled around and came up behind her partner.

Flint's eyes narrowed, matching the gaze of the imposing shark-shifter, Drego. Behind him, the arena floor dropped away into a deep body of water—Drego's primary advantage. With a swift, focused motion, Flint pressed his hands together, channeling his earth magic. The arena floor shuddered, and a formidable wall of rock shot upwards, dividing the dry land from the surging waters. Drego, now half-submerged, bared his sharp, gleaming teeth and lunged toward Flint, as the water behind him churned into a furious whirlpool.

Each snap of Drego's jaws tested Flint's reflexes as he deftly dodged the attacks, his feet firmly planted on the dry earth. The whirlpool intensified with each thrash of Drego's powerful tail, its pull growing stronger, but Flint stood his ground. His earth magic vibrated through the rocky barrier, reinforcing it against the onslaught of water. Flint's lungs heaved and his pulse raced, matching the rhythm of the crashing waves and the echo of his own resolve.

Flint smirked, his eyes gleaming with mischief. "Hey, Drego! Your shark bite needs some work. Maybe I can give you some pointers after this?"

Drego snarled, a hint of amusement in his voice.

"Keep talking, Flint. It'll make it even sweeter when I sink my teeth into victory."

Orion turned his attention to Zara on the other side of the arena, fire swirling around her hands in a hypnotizing dance as she prepared to counterattack her own challenger. The air crackled with anticipation as Zara and the elegant movements of Naga, the snake-shifter girl, faced off.

Zara unleashed twin orbs of fire at Naga who, with a snake-like grace, dodged the blazing attacks. The air wavered with their heat. Sensing her moment, Zara intensified her fire magic, her hands glowing like the heart of a furnace. In an explosive display, she sent a roaring wave of fire at her adversary. The air snapped and sparked as the fiery onslaught met snake magic, casting dancing shadows across the battleground.

Orion watched the Fantasia students, their movements quick and confident. They faced Flint and Zara without hesitation, making Orion's stomach churn with anxiety. The tournament demanded much, both physically and magically. He tightened his grip, silently vowing to stand by his friends, just as they always stood by him.

He leaned against the stone wall, his gaze fixed on the arena where their friends were engaged in a fierce battle. Elara stood beside him, her hands clenched.

"They're going all out," Orion commented, his voice brimming with excitement and a hint of worry. "Flint's rocking it with his earth manipulation, but Drego's shark shifting skills are giving him an advantage."

Elara nodded, her eyes focused on Zara's fiery onslaught. "And check out Zara! Her fire magic is fierce, but Naga's slithery agility is keeping her on her toes. I'm glad it's not me."

As the fight intensified, Orion felt a surge of adrenaline. "Right, but we're up next," he said. "We need to be ready, Elara. Our friends are giving it their all, and we can't let the school down. Everyone has worked so hard to get this far."

Elara watched the intense battle unfold. "You're right, Orion. We've trained for this. Let's show them what we're capable of and give them a fight they won't forget!"

In the Fantasia School section, mermaid students with glistening scales cheered with haunting melodies, while animal-shifters transformed and added growls and hoots to the mix, their cheers and boos morphing into various creatures.

While Flint valiantly defended himself against Drego's unyielding onslaught, Zara seized the perfect moment. With a burst of energy, she propelled herself into the air, her legs driving her forward with astonishing force. Flames engulfed her, forming a blazing cloak that radiated intense heat, a stark juxtaposition to the frigid atmosphere of the arena.

Flint's attention momentarily shifted when he glanced over at Zara, his eyes widening with both awe and concern.

"Flint! Watch out!" Orion shouted from the sidelines.

Drego seized his opportunity. With a burst of speed and agility, he lunged at Flint. Powerful muscles rippled beneath his skin as Drego closed in on Flint, ready to unleash his formidable shark-like abilities.

"Flint!" Elara yelled, as she watched from the sidelines.

But it was too late. The shark-shifter's razor-sharp teeth sank into Flint's torso, breaking through his protective earth barrier and ripping his Charmcaster Academy uniform. The impact sent Flint crashing to the arena floor, leaving a trail of crimson blood in his wake.

"Flint!" Elara gasped, her hand covering her mouth in shock as she watched their friend struggle to rise.

Orion felt his heart racing, his pulse hammering in his ears as he stared at the gruesome injury Flint received.

Zara and Naga stopped battling and made their way over to Drego and Flint. Professor Swiftwater ran out of the alcove and into the arena.

"Medics! We need medics now!" Elara shouted, her voice cracking with urgency.

The clamor of the crowd seemed to fade into a distant hum as two figures clad in white uniforms dashed onto the battlefield. They moved with practiced efficiency, their faces etched with grim expressions. Several Charmcasters in paramedic uniforms ran onto the battlefield to tend to Flint. Two more emerged from a hidden wall and brought out a stretcher.

"Unbelievable! The animal shifter from Fantasia has dealt a devastating blow to Charmcaster Academy's Flint!" the announcer's voice boomed the bad news throughout the arena, echoing off the walls and reverberating in Orion's chest.

The spectators reacted with a mixture of shock, awe, and horror, their faces reflecting their allegiance to their respective schools. Fantasia students leaped from their seats, cheering and jeering, while Charmcaster supporters looked on in disbelief and dismay. Even Headmistress Nightshade seemed taken aback, her normally stoic expression betraying a flicker of concern.

Orion clenched his fists tightly, feeling his nails dig into his palms. This can't be happening, he thought, his mind reeling as he tried to make sense of what he'd just witnessed. How could Flint have been so easily defeated? What did this mean for the rest of their team —and for their chances in the tournament?

"Poor Flint," Elara whispered, her wide eyes meeting Orion's. "I hope he's okay."

"He will be. He has to be," Orion said, swallowing hard. "Flint is strong."

Orion blinked rapidly, as if trying to dispel a nightmare, but the scene before him remained unaltered. Flint lay crumpled on the ground, blood oozing from a deep gash that marred his cheek. Orion's breath hitched, catching painfully in his throat.

"Flint will be okay," he told himself again, attempting to quell the rising panic within. "He's tough. He'll pull through."

But the words rang hollow, doing little to soothe his fears. A crushing sense of responsibility weighed heavily upon him.

Orion watched, his gaze locked on Flint, as the medics carefully lifted him onto a stretcher. They worked swiftly and silently, securing him with straps before hoisting the stretcher up between them.

As the paramedics carried him away, Flint's eyes

met Orion's for a brief moment—eyes filled with pain, but also trust. He lifted his arm and gave the crowd a thumb's up. The audience clamored to their feet and thunderous applause filled the stadium. Zara went with Flint, holding his hand and waving to the crowd.

"I think he's going to be just fine," Elara said, gripping his arm tightly. "We're up next."

"Right," he replied, taking a deep breath and summoning every ounce of courage he possessed. He squared his shoulders. "We've got this, Elara. For Flint. For Charmcaster Academy."

"Time to show off our skills," Elara said, her voice steady and strong.

"Oh, yeah! Those students are going down," Orion agreed, his eyes blazing.

Together, they stepped onto the battlefield, the roar of the crowd resounding in their ears like a battle cry. A potent mix of fear and revenge fueled Orion. He knew they faced great danger—perhaps even greater than they had initially expected—but he also knew that he would not back down.

CHAPTER TWENTY

As Orion and Elara stood side by side, ready to face whatever challenges the Otherworld Triad Tournament had in store for them next, Orion knew one thing: they would not go down without a fight.

"Get ready for the grand finale!" The announcer's voice exploded across the arena, electrifying the air. "Representing Fantasia School, here come our fierce competitors! Meet Cressida Merewin, a siren from the deep. Her command of water magic is unparalleled, leaving her foes in her turbulent wake! And at her side, the enigmatic Talbot Lycanstein, a werewolf whose fortitude is as sharp as his fangs!"

Fantasia School's spectators erupted in deafening applause as the pair entered the battlefield. Glistening mermaid tails shot into the air like fireworks, creating a kaleidoscope of colorful sea spray, while a shapeshifter roared as a mighty lion.

Cressida seemed almost surreal. She was tall, with silver eyes that had a glow of their own, like moonlight reflecting off a calm sea. Her pink hair fell freely around her shoulders, and they clad her in a loose-flowing outfit of midnight blue that danced and swirled like smoke every time she moved.

Alongside her, Talbot stood out in stark contrast. He was a tall with broad shoulders, an intimidating figure—a real-life werewolf. His face was hidden in the shadow of a dark hood, his eyes unreadable. Orion felt a hint of apprehension as he eyed Talbot's broad, muscular form.

The announcer's voice electrified the air and echoed off every corner of the massive stadium. "Now introducing from Charmcaster Academy, Orion Evergreen! He's not your typical green thumb! This lad commands plants with a finesse that's downright remarkable!" A boisterous cheer rippled through the crowd. "And partnering him, we have Elara Silverwind! With her breath, she doesn't just blow out candles, she summons gales! A caster of wind magic like you've never seen before!"

The audience roared their approval, the energy in the stands reaching a fever pitch.

Orion's fists tightened, his veins buzzing with an earthy energy as he connected with the very life force of the plants beneath his feet. Beside him, Elara's eyes gleamed with a sharp focus, the air humming around her in anticipation as she summoned her command over the wind.

With a loud howl that bounced off the arena walls, the werewolf boy attacked first. Talbot, embodying the fearsome agility of his werewolf nature, lunged forward. His muscled form, a blur of motion, darted across the field, his predatory eyes locked onto Orion and Elara.

A savage growl erupted from Talbot's throat as he launched himself toward them. His claws swiped through the air, carving deadly arcs that intimidated and wound.

But Orion and Elara were a step ahead. Agile and swift, they used their wind and plant magic, and their combined efforts transformed the battlefield into an electrifying stage of pulsating energy and nimble foot-work, a testament to their shared determination and survival instincts.

Cressida's eyes glowed a dangerous blue, and with a graceful, sinuous movement that was terrifyingly swift, she advanced. As she moved, a stream of water formed around her, twisting and turning with a life of its own. It surged forward, an angry aquatic arrow aimed directly at Orion and Elara.

"Stay back, water witch!" Orion's voice echoed through the tumult, raw power pulsing in his words.

His arms swept out wide, his connection to everything green and growing beneath the arena's floor flared to life. Thick vines, pulsing with raw energy, erupted from the ground in response. They coiled and twisted in the air, creating a writhing botanical barrier between Cressida's watery assault and their vulnerable forms. With a snap of Orion's fingers, they lunged forward, aiming to ensnare the aquatic predator before she could unleash her fury.

Just as the vines lunged toward Cressida, Elara moved into action. Orion knew that her connection with the wind was as innate as breathing, her magic an unbroken song that swirled around her, vibrant and alive. Elara took a deep breath, and the wind responded, gathering around her in a violent vortex. With a swift motion of her hands, she directed the gale-force winds toward Talbot, intending to blast the werewolf off balance. With the werewolf stuck in a tornado of wind that lifted him off the ground, Elara joined Orion to fight the mermaid.

The arena filled with the bellowing noise of the wind colliding with the water around Cressida, sending plumes of spray high into the air. A full-fledged hurricane.

Orion watched Elara, awe-struck, as she relentlessly drove her magic forward. Wind tangled her hair into a wild halo, a testament to her fight to create an opening for him. Gritting her teeth, she launched another gust, stronger and more forceful, hurdling towards Cressida. Orion's heart pounded in sync with her efforts. He knew this was his moment to strike.

Even as the winds lashed around her, Cressida met the storm head-on. Her eyes glinted with a predatory gleam as she steadied herself, her connection with the water around her lending her an uncanny balance. Raising her hands, she channeled her own magic, the water in the arena surging at her command, dampening the force of Elara's winds.

Orion pressed forward, fingers digging into the soil as he willed the plant life beneath the arena floor to answer his call. Vines erupted from the ground, snaking toward Cressida, aiming to ensnare her. But the mermaid proved too nimble, her movements fluid and graceful, effortlessly evading the onslaught of the creeping vegetation.

With a flick of her wrist, Cressida summoned a

torrent of water, which collided with the vines, dousing Orion's efforts to detain her. The mermaid's triumphant laugh echoed around the arena as she deftly avoided both Orion and Elara's combined attacks, her strength and agility proving too much for them.

"Orion, I can't hold her off much longer! And keep Talbot suspended in my cyclone too!" Elara cried, desperation lacing her voice as she narrowly dodged another brutal swipe from Cressida.

As Elara danced with the wind, she redirected its ferocity toward Cressida. Her palms faced forward, shooting a tempest force wind that whipped up debris and dust, obscuring vision. Yet Cressida only smirked, her lithe form dipping and bending with the onslaught like a reed in a river.

"We need a new plan," Orion said urgently, his gaze darting around the arena. A patch of bramble and thornbushes caught his eye, their prickly menace an idea in the making. "Elara, try to steer her toward those thorns!"

Without missing a beat, Elara adjusted her winds, pushing at Cressida from different angles, guiding her toward the brambles. Cressida laughed, her powerful legs adapting to the force, but the mirth in her eyes began to fade as she saw the thorn-ridden trap looming ahead.

Just as Elara directed Cressida into the path of the brambles, Orion struck. His voice a command in the wild cacophony of battle, he called upon the earth; the brambles responding to his command. The thorny tendrils erupted upwards, snaking toward the mermaid in a prickly wave, poised to ensnare her.

Orion glanced up. The crowd seemed to hold their breath, anticipation stunting the air.

He felt a momentary wave of victory as he saw his brambles trapping Cressida. Her frustrated snarl was quickly drowned by the gasps from the crowd. But victory was short-lived as a growl echoed throughout the arena.

Talbot, the formidable werewolf, was on the move and free of Elara's wind magic, and the sight of his entrapped teammate seemed to have triggered a burst of anger. His fangs glistened in the arena lights, and his eyes focused on Orion and Elara like a hunter zeroing in on its prey.

"Ready?" Orion said, locking eyes with Elara.

"Born ready," Elara said with a fierce grin.

As Talbot lunged, they sprang into action, their movements synchronized through countless hours of practice. Orion swerved, his feet barely skimming the ground as he used his plant magic to whip up a shield of thick, interwoven branches. Elara, on the other hand, threw her arms wide, summoning a gust of wind that pushed against the oncoming werewolf. The two elements clashed with Talbot's force, creating a spectacle that had the crowd gasping, their hearts thundering in their chests like war drums.

Even with the vines and the wind fighting against him, Talbot continued his relentless attack. His werewolf strength allowed him to plow through Orion's shield of branches, snapping them like they were mere twigs.

During the chaos, Orion spotted an opening. He manipulated the roots beneath the arena floor to trip Talbot, and for a split second, the werewolf stumbled.

"Orion, now!" she yelled.

Reacting on instinct, Orion forced every ounce of his power into the plant life beneath them, making them grow rapidly. Massive vines sprung from the ground, wrapping around Talbot and halting his charge.

Meanwhile, Elara raised her hands, palms facing the sky, and called upon her wind magic. A whirlwind formed around her, spiraling upward and gaining speed with every passing second. Then, with a quick slash of her hands, she sent the whirlwind hurling toward Talbot. The werewolf roared as the wind slammed into him, knocking him off his feet and sending him skidding across the arena.

Even while constrained, Talbot was gnashing his teeth, readying for another lunge. And Cressida, although hindered, was already tearing through the vines, her eyes flashing fiercely as she re-focused on her targets.

Orion and Elara had only gained a moment of respite.

"Enough!" Orion declared, reaching deep within himself to draw on every ounce of strength he possessed.

His veins pulsed with an innate power, the life-force of all plant-life echoing his mighty power. Then Orion roared—a primal, defiant bellow that reverberated throughout the arena. In response, the earth shivered beneath their feet. From the very heart of the battlefield, a huge vine erupted. Its monstrous tendrils shot out like lightning, lashing toward Talbot and Cressida.

The vine was relentless, untamed, mirroring Orion's raw resolve. It coiled around the pair in a cruel imitation of a serpent's deadly embrace. There was no escape—the thorny behemoth was too fast, too powerful. The once formidable opponents were now caught hopelessly ensnared. Their struggles were futile against the unstoppable might of Orion's unleashed power.

The final echoes of battle subsided, replaced by the rapid hammering of Orion's heartbeat in his ears. His knees buckled beneath him, finding solace in the cool, firm ground. Elara tumbled beside him, her chest heaving in ragged synchrony with his. Exhaustion draped over them like a heavy shroud.

"Charmcaster Academy takes the victory!" The announcer's voice boomed across the noisy arena.

The crowd's frenzied cheers built into a crescendo. The reality of their triumph wove through Orion's weariness, igniting a spark of joy.

He turned to Elara, their eyes meeting in a shared moment of triumph and relief. Both were panting, faces flushed, but their eyes were alight with the embers of triumph. They had battled with everything they had —for Flint, for their school, for each other. And they had triumphed.

"Let's get out of here," Elara suggested, her voice shaking slightly. She attempted a smirk, the corner of her lips twitching weakly. "We've got some celebrating to do. Don't you think we've earned some victory pizza by now?"

Orion chuckled, fatigue coloring his laughter with a husky tone. "My favorite! I'll race you to it," Orion retorted, grinning through his fatigue as he offered her a supportive hand, leading them out of the battlefield. Both walking a little slower than they did earlier in the day.

They limped into the waiting area under the arena, where Headmistress Nightshade appeared within a whirl of celestial light.

"Orion, Elara," Headmistress Nightshade said, her voice soft but filled with the weight of their accomplishment. "The courage, the tenacity, the raw talent four showcased today...it's not just noteworthy. It's extraordinary." She stood tall and proud.

And for the first time since they had arrived at Charmcaster Academy, both teens truly believed in themselves.

Orion's adrenaline was still doing a full-on victory dance. As his grin spread, he thought about the kid he used to be, all nerves and self-doubt when he first stepped through Charmcaster Academy's doors. Now, the surge of pride knocking at his ribcage was something he could get used to. This, he decided, was what a 'big' win felt like.

"Can you believe it, Elara? We actually did it!" Orion exclaimed, grinning.

"I knew we would win," Elara replied, her eyes sparkling. "Because we make a great team, Orion."

His smile grew as he looked at Elara with gratitude; she had always believed in him, just like his family, even when he didn't believe in himself.

"You're my best friend, Elara," he said softly.

She bumped her shoulder into his. "Of course I am."

They briefly hugged and laughed.

Then Orion grew serious and looked at the headmistress. "Will Flint be okay?"

Headmistress Nightshade's stern expression softened into a rare smile. "Of course," she said. "He's with our most powerful healers and should be fine in a couple of days. Now, students, come with me."

They followed her back to the arena. All the plants and the opposing teams were gone. The flooring was a hard marble floor now, their footsteps echoed off the smooth surface as they moved to the center. Zara appeared and joined them. She shook Orion's hand and gave Elara a brief hug.

Headmistress Nightshade cleared her throat, drawing the attention of the surrounding students and professors. "Students of Charmcaster Academy, today we have witnessed an incredible display of skill, courage, and teamwork by our students," she declared, her voice thundering throughout the arena. "Orion, Elara, Zara, and Flint have made us all proud by winning the Otherworld Triad Tournament for our school. Orion and Elara have also thwarted a dangerous attempt to expose the magical world by outing Professor Mistrial's murderer."

The crowd erupted into cheers. Once more, showering the victorious students with admiration and praise.

Headmistress Nightshade continued in a booming voice, "In recognition of their extraordinary achievements beyond the tournament, I am honored to present Orion and Elara with the prestigious Charmcaster Crest."

She produced two gleaming silver medallions from the pocket of her robes, each etched with intricate designs, including the school's emblem. The headmistress placed medallions around their necks, her eyes full of pride.

"Not only have you shown great honor, but your past actions have also safeguarded our world," she said, her voice filled with admiration as she addressed them directly. "You've truly proven yourselves as exceptional Charmcasters, and I couldn't be prouder."

"Thank you, Headmistress Nightshade," Orion replied, his voice choked with emotion.

He glanced at Elara, who was beaming, happy tears glistening in her eyes.

As the cheers continued, Orion thought of his family. He had finally made them proud, and his heart swelled. Standing beside Elara, their hard-earned medallions gleaming in the sunlight, Orion knew this was just the beginning of their journey as Charmcasters—a journey filled with magic, adventure, and unbreakable friendships.

THANK-YOU FOR READING BOOK 1 IN THE YA Series, Charmcaster Academy. Stay Tuned for Book 2 from the students of Charmcaster Academy.

ABOUT THE AUTHOR

Georgia-based writer Manswell T. Peterson's sequential series is taking the paranormal genre by storm! In bringing the Locrottum Universe to life, Manswell becomes the first African American male author to create an entire universe in the paranormal genre. The Locrottum princess and bride books are the first six in his 200+ adult book series.

Manswell has been writing since the fifth grade, using the craft as a cathartic tool to cope with and escape from the harsh reality of growing up with a mother battling serious drug addiction. He fondly tells readers, "I didn't go pro in sports; I went pro in writing!

Manswell has been writing professionally since 2008, having authored 50 books with more than 300,000 copies sold, and developed screenplays for dozens of movies and television shows.

It took Manswell a decade to fully create the Locrottum Universe. The Universe includes 200 books and more than 500 characters! Think Fast & The Furious, Twilight, Star Wars, and Harry Potter all in one!

Manswell has also developed the Locrottum Academy book series for young adults (ages 13+) to introduce young readers to the paranormal world. He is well on his way to claiming the crown of the "King of Paranormal."

He is the former Department Chair and Instructor of Criminal Justice at Darton State College. He is married to his lovely wife, Dr. Latonya Peterson. They have two sons, Manswell II and Braylen. He is a disabled Navy Veteran and a proud member of Omega Psi Phi Fraternity, Inc.